BELIEVING IN MARVELS

SARAH M BAILEY

Produced with the support of Creative New Zealand

First published in 2021 by Betty & Ida Books

ISBN 978 0 473 57011 8 (paperback)
ISBN 978 0 473 57012 5 (epub)
ISBN 978 0 73 57013 2 (kindle)
ISBN 978 0473 57014 9 (PDF)
ISBN 978 0 73 57015 6 (ibook)

A catalogue record for this book is available from the National Library of New Zealand.

Cover and internal design: Cheryl Smith (macarndesign.com)

In memory of my high school
English teacher, Mr G McCorry
— I got there in the end.

CHAPTER ONE

I tap my watch, curse its stopped hands and brace for the inevitable. It's too late to turn back. A swarm of green shirts surrounds me and I'm a speck of blue denim in the middle. Maybe if I merge with this group of juniors in front, my ex-classmates won't spot me. Here goes: head down, fast pace, avoid eye contact.

"Weirdo." A gang of girls jostles me, shooting nasty looks and squelching gum.

The vision dulls the insult, it's unusually bright and insistent, leaving dazzling white haloes everywhere. A vaguely familiar boy flashes before me, he trips over and there's a lot of blood. By the time the image has faded, the girls are ahead, smiling over their shoulders at a loose-limbed boy sauntering along: the boy from my vision.

Heart-sinking revelation hits me—he goes to my new school. I cover my face and stop dead. Elbows shove me. A male voice swears into my ear, making me jump. To my right someone hoicks up phlegm then spits; the slimy liquid dribbles down my leg and I shiver. My feet glue to the pavement as dread battles with my conscience.

The hum of chatter and scuffle of bodies subside.

A scream cuts the air. I let in a chink of light through my trembling fingers. *Oh God, no.*

"Let me through, please." Breathing hard, I push against the crowd of people surrounding the tree, muscle my way through the three-deep throng, then stagger free and into a pool of blood.

"I'm so sorry, it's all my f—" I look up into soft brown eyes and glimpse a glowing white aura around him. Behind me, laughter drowns out my words. I swallow and keep my back to the spectators.

"Sorry? Didn't watch where I was going." The boy's voice is weak, his brow slick with sweat. He winces and clutches his leg, twisting his head away from the blood.

I pull off my hoody and apply pressure around the wound to stem the bleeding.

"Marvel, you freak. We already called an ambulance," a girl mutters. Her words drip with contempt.

The injured boy glances in the direction of the girl's voice and frowns.

"It's okay, I'm used to it." My face is hot and I feel his eyes on me. I move his bag away from the blood, untangle his headphones from thick brown curls and loop them around his neck, anything rather than let him see my tears.

Faint sirens break through the hubbub. They grow louder, making my ears ring, then stop. Blue light flashes against the tree trunk and across the boy's face. Tyres crunch gravel followed by radio crackle and doors opening.

"I'll stay with you. It's the least I can do." I place a hand on his and meet his eyes. "I'm Marvel. What's your name?"

"Noa." He squeezes my hand. "Thanks, Marvel."

Paramedics swoop in and take over. One of them gives me back my bloodied hoody. I glance behind and exhale; the crowd has dispersed.

A paramedic mentions fracture, mumbles about an operation.

I gasp, step back and jerk my gaze over their heads to Noa's wide eyes.

"Can I go with him?" My voice pleads.

"No, sorry, love, we'll phone his family. Thanks for your help—good thinking with the hoody, eased the bleeding." His voice is calm, composed, like bone sticking out of a boy's ankle is no drama.

A lump forms in my throat. I rush over and grab Noa's hand where it hangs limply over one side of the stretcher. "I'm really, really sorry."

He lifts his head up, confusion in his eyes. "Why?"

"I, err …" I look away, let Noa's hand drop and try to hold back tears.

I wait by the ambulance doors, watching the flurry of activity inside and clutch my sticky, blood-stained hands together. Guilt pumps through my veins like an adrenaline surge I can't burn off.

Doors slam shut. The ambulance hurtles down the street, bouncing over the speed bumps I love to skate and leaves me standing alone in a cloud of exhaust fumes.

Behind me, by the errant tree root that caused his fall, is Noa's backpack. I hurl it over my shoulder and drag my heavy heart home.

I trudge up the wooden steps to Sadie's door, lean my forehead against the cool paintwork and ring the bell. My shoulders ache. Heavy backpacks slide down each arm and slump against decking. Under the shelter of Sadie's verandah, still air fills with the metallic smell of blood.

"Good Lord, what on earth happened?" Sadie clamps a hand over her mouth. "Is this *your* blood?"

I shake my head and try to speak. My chest heaves and fat tears soak into my bloody shirt, forming translucent rust-coloured rings.

Sadie wraps her arm around my waist and guides me inside.

The hallway's warm and smells of furniture polish. I stand in a shaft of sunlight, transfixed by glittering dust motes while Sadie divests me of bags, skateboard and bloody clothes, then wraps me in a scratchy towel. For a few seconds I'm a little kid again, clambering out of Sadie's claw foot bath into the towel stretched between her arms. My lip trembles and I pull away from Sadie's fumbling hands, tuck the towel ends around my chest and close the bathroom door behind me.

I take a sip of sweet tea. The delicate china cup clinks against its saucer in my unsteady hand. I lean forward and meet my grandmother's eyes. "Why did I inherit this? It's not a Gift at all, it's a curse." I thump the arm of the couch and Sadie startles. "This Year Thirteen, Noa, needs surgery. He's scarred for life. All because of me." I hold back tears. "Visions, visions, every day now, weird stuff, pictures flashing up of stupid shit: a skull ring, a playground, then I see him fall, so clear and bright, and, and …" I falter. China rattles with the rise and fall of my quivering breath. I screw my eyes up tight. "And, I didn't warn him."

"Oh my dear Marvella, don't be so hard on yourself. Sometimes you make the wrong call." Sadie unfurls my fingers from the cup and saucer and places them on the coffee table. Her warm hand takes mine. "Adolescence was tough for your Aunt Shirley, too. The channels are open, you're vulnerable. Don't despair, meaning will come." She hesitates. "*I know.*"

I glare into her pale blue eyes. "What kind of knowing?" I've told her a million times about this. Knowing isn't straightforward; there are degrees, ranging from simple claircognisance to the way more reliable precognitive.

Sadie waves me away. "Goodness, I've no idea, can't abide those technical terms. Knowing is knowing."

I sigh and look down.

"Hmm, not sure. Should I?" Sadie mutters. She stares out the window. "Yes, maybe telling her now might help, make her feel better." She turns to me, gives a tight smile.

"What?" I sit up straight.

She takes a deep breath. "You're going to save your cousin."

My insides churn. I'm actually going to help someone? I perch on the edge of the couch. "Really?"

"Absolutely."

Her conviction allows me a rare moment of hope, that after all these years, something useful may come from being psychic.

"So, I thought you should meet him again and, well, a haircut wouldn't go amiss." She passes me an envelope. "Do you remember Vince?" She meets my eyes and bites her lip.

"Vaguely. He used to come over when I was a little kid. Dad kept telling him to piss off."

Sadie looks down. "Yes, that sounds like something your father would say." She pauses. "It's complicated."

I tear open the envelope. The card inside reads: Bad Hair Daze—Vince Allen. If there's one thing I dislike more than being psychic, it's getting my hair cut.

"Why the salon? Can't he just come here?"

"If your father sees him, he'll be very upset. You know how he is. He flies off the handle if I even mention Vince. And, your hair ..." Sadie sighs, tugs at the string of pearls around her neck.

I couldn't care less about all the knots and split ends but saving someone, well, that would be like winning gold at the X Games. I pitch back against the couch and close my eyes. The card's sharp corners dig into my palm. "Okay. I'll do it."

Her face relaxes. She collects my empty cup and looks at me. "What are you going to do about the boy?"

Guilt jolts me and Noa's frightened face flashes up. "Might go see him tomorrow, return his bag." The words flow out instinctively—shouldn't I think this through first?

Sadie stares vacantly through the lounge window as if cogs in her mind are slowly revolving. She smiles at the glass. "That sounds like a very good idea."

Before I can ask why, she turns on her heels. Her patent leather shoes click against the shiny wooden floor, the same shoes in which I paraded across these floors as a child, my tiny feet barely filling the toes. I stare at Sadie's bent spine, noticing how her head and neck crane through the kitchen door ahead of it.

Her words come back to me: *You're going to save your cousin.* It's the most certain she's been in seventeen years. I clutch my head in my hands. If only I had saved Noa, too.

CHAPTER TWO

I clench the strap of Noa's backpack, take a deep breath and try to slow my thumping heart. Beige hospital walls surround me and the stink of disinfectant burns my eyes. A nurse rushes past, turning off a beeping machine, and, ahead, an elderly man shuffles along with a walking frame, his dressing-gown cord trailing behind over stained brown carpet.

I stop by the entrance to a four-bedded bay. Doubt descends like a deluge of Auckland summer rain. What if he thinks I'm a joke, too, and it spreads around my new school? The bloodstain on his backpack catches my eye and I swallow hard; the least I owe him is an explanation.

Noa's scored the bed by the window, the only patient without a visitor. His leg rests on a pillow, encased in a cast below his knee. His beautiful white aura draws me like a magnet.

A slow smile forms as he sees me.

"Hi. I brought your bag. I tried to get the blood

out." Heat spreads across my cheeks. I place his bag against the wall, roll my skateboard under the bed and wipe my sweaty palms over the back of my jeans. I grab a plastic chair, glance at his leg and shudder. "I'm so sorry—I feel terrible."

"Why?" His voice is gentle, not a grain of hostility in it.

I lift my eyes to his, hesitating, dwelling in this moment before the truth is out, before he knows I'm not like any other girl he's ever met. Before my new start's ruined. I take a deep inhale. "I'm psychic and I predicted your fall."

Noa smiles and my heart sinks. He presses down on his hands, heaves himself up against the stack of pillows. "Wow! That's awesome."

I stare at him, shaking my head. "You broke your ankle. If I'd warned you …"

"Don't stress about it, accidents happen."

I sink my gaze, intent on the tiny dents and scratches on the floor's surface to focus my stunned brain. A machine whirrs over the drone of low chatter around me. Guilt lifts and I'm weightless, like flying through the air after skating up a speed bump, all my earthly worries forgotten in that few seconds of pure freedom. I look up. "I wanted a fresh start—a new school—ignore the visions, but—"

He cuts me off. "You go to Western High?"

"Enrolled a few weeks back. Left St Joseph's—the bullying got pretty bad."

His eyes widen. "Did they know you could see the future?"

"I warned people. They'd just laugh, then after it happened, they'd turn on me."

He shakes his head and tuts.

I'm so taken aback by his sympathy, I blurt out the whole sorry tale: how visions flash up most days like daydreams, how I used to block them with doodling, counting in my head and then, as I got older, skateboarding. I tell him about unheeded warnings, like when Albert Liu, the sweet Chinese man from down the road walked into a lamp post; a few basic words of Mandarin weren't much use in preventing his accident.

He laughs at that anecdote, then stops and looks embarrassed. "Must be tough."

Emotion washes over me. *Don't cry in front of him, don't be pathetic.* "Yeah." I sink my head.

Noa grabs my arm. "What about Lotto, can you predict it?"

I meet his bright eyes and prepare to dash his hopes. "It doesn't work like that."

His smile falls. "Oh, well, worth asking." He glances out the window and mumbles, "People who need it most never win."

The playground image pops up. It's like a film clip above my head, only a few seconds, then gone. Two giggling kids wearing raincoats swing against a grey sky. The playground sits at the far end of a large recreational area surrounded by terraces of new homes. As visions go it's quite pleasant, preferable to ones where someone gets hurt.

"You went into a trance—did you see something?" Noa's voice is high.

My face grows hot. Voices in the room fall silent.

"Yes." I keep it low, hoping the other people can't hear. "Some kids at a playground."

"Oh." He looks disappointed.

"Better than seeing an accident …"

Noa winces. "Sorry. I bet boring ones are just fine."

I tilt my head and debate whether to say more. The kindness in his eyes reassures me. "Sadie, my grandmother, predicts I'm going to save my long-lost cousin." I give a light laugh and cross the fingers of both hands.

Noa pushes curls off his face. "Sheesh. Is your whole family like you?"

"Sadie just does palms. I'm psychic, so was Aunt Shirley—she died before I was born." I pause. God, I haven't asked Noa anything and he's the one in hospital. He must think I'm so wrapped up in myself. "Is your surname Salesa? I think I saw one of your paintings up in B4, a portrait?"

"Yeah, that's my dad." He swallows and turns to me like he wants to say something, then shifts his gaze to the bedsheet.

"What is it?" I say softly.

"He died. Liver cancer." His voice is a whisper.

I want to sink through the floor. "I'm so sorry."

"I've been the main man since I was fifteen." Noa stares ahead while his front teeth graze his lower lip. He wipes a hand across his eyes. "Sorry. I didn't mean to burden you."

I hold his gaze and neither of us says anything.

He breaks the silence. "I'm out of here in a few days, once they're happy with the wound and I can use these without falling over." He nods to the crutches stacked by the window. "Maybe we can hang out after school?"

I grip the sides of the chair. "I'd like that."

◆

I jump off my board and climb the steep hill towards home with a lightness in my feet and a warm glow inside me. In the distance, over pitched rooftops, the sun dips behind Taylor's Hill, creating an arc of golden sky above the treeline.

A text beeps. It's Mum asking where I am. I frown at the time on my phone and cold dread grips me; my watch is out by half an hour. A cloud blots out the distant arc of sunlight and the sky above me darkens. The wind picks up, sending sharp leaves circling around my feet, ditching them in gaps beneath the hedge bordering the pavement. I run; try and hold off the vision until I reach home but it's too late. The skull ring reappears and I sink to my knees. It dominates my field of vision, its gritted gleaming teeth so close it's like they're going to bite. Bright light reflects off the skull's ruby eyes showering red haloes everywhere I look. There's a horrid smell like the air is doused in bleach but ten times stronger and so fumy my eyes smart. As I breathe this caustic air my throat burns and tightens. I screw up my eyes and shout at it to go away. Nausea overwhelms me and, between retches, I snatch another poisonous breath, feeling my throat close even tighter. It's hard to breathe now and black spots obscure the vision, then everything around me blurs.

The air calms. A wind chime tinkles from behind the hedge; the only proof of a disturbance.

I inhale fresh air. *Twice in one week. What weird shit is this?* I press trembling fingers against my pulsing temples, but meaning doesn't come. I crawl to the hedge, grasp its prickly foliage and haul myself up.

Another text pings in from Mum: *Darling, I'm beside myself*, followed by a broken heart emoji. I pick up pace, texting as I go and tell her I missed the bus. I'm not stopping for anyone.

As I run flat out to the top of the street, skateboard under one arm, Sadie's white villa passes in a blur to my left, her low box hedge a haze of green. My street intersects with the main road and levels off. I drop my board, take a right and pound concrete so hard my foot hurts. Wheels roll faster over smooth pavement and my fear crumbles; I'm back in control.

My confidence growing, I ollie off the kerb and weave a graceful, sweeping S-shape down an empty side street. Accelerating towards the speed bump, momentum lifts me, wheels revolving through air before smacking onto the asphalt again. I slow as the street inclines upwards, but I'm restless; it's not long enough—not for this vision. No way am I heading home yet. I need to be sated; to know for certain it won't come back again tonight.

♦

Mum springs from the couch, bangles clanging down her slim wrists and wraps her arms around me. She smells of turps. "It's almost eight. You look exhausted." She tugs my skateboard from my hands. Dirt from its wheels marks her shirt, dulling the bright paint splatters.

Dad beckons for me to sit in his favourite chair.

I slump into it and close my eyes. My muscles ache but my mind is calm and settled.

Fierce whispers carry over from the kitchen.

Dad's gruff voice. "She's never stayed out this long before, she's been gone hours. Damn spirits must be hassling her."

Mum strikes a more positive tone. "We can only support her, as we've always done. She's tough, like Shirley was."

"No benevolent spirit warned Shirley cancer

would take her at thirty-four. All seems a bit one-sided to me." He bangs a mug onto the countertop, slams the cupboard door and clicks on the kettle.

Dad walks over and kneels beside me. He places his broad hand on mine. "You okay?"

I force a smile. "Had a bad one, but I feel better now."

My gaze drifts to the kitchen, where Mum's loading the dishwasher.

Dad clears his throat. "Good to hear." He places a small stack of CDs into my lap. "The best of American Lo-fi."

I see hope in his eyes and sigh. "Thanks."

Dad believes music is therapy; that it'll focus my mind and prevent the visions coming through. I feel the weight of the CDs in my lap. The only thing they're going to give me is a headache.

"This one's been a pleasant distraction from the Dark Web." He stretches out his arm and holds up one of the CDs. The monochrome face on his Misfits T-shirt straightens out.

Of all his band T-shirts, I don't mind this one. Those with tour dates on the back are the worst: ancient and faded and way too tight over his belly.

"You wouldn't believe the horrors for sale on the Dark Web." He shakes his head. "It's the devil's supermarket."

I cringe and hold a palm to his face. "Dad, I don't want to know."

If there's a hidden corner of society, Dad will write an article about it. Underbellies and subcultures are his speciality.

"How was the hospital? Grubby and understaffed?"

I frown. "He's home soon on crutches."

"You tell him?"

I nod.

"And?" Dad's knees click as he stands. He yanks up the waistband of his black jeans.

"He seems to believe me." My voice cracks and a rush of emotion overcomes me.

"That's a first." He looks me straight in the eye. "He, Marvel, is a keeper—you want to hold onto him."

Don't worry, I intend to.

CHAPTER THREE

I press my back against the hall brickwork to avoid the horde of students heading for the gate. The brick's rough surface scrapes my arms, so I take a step higher and scan the crowd for Noa. My hands tighten into sweaty fists and I take slow deep breaths. *Where is he?* Probably having second thoughts. Though no one at Western High has shouted *freak, devil worshipper* or *weirdo* in my direction, or dropped stones in the path of my skateboard since we last spoke.

A distant clicking sound grows louder and Noa's in front of me with a crutch wedged under each arm.

He smiles. "Hey, how's it going?" Beads of sweat glisten across his forehead.

My cheeks heat. "You're here."

He looks puzzled, then glances over to the road beyond the school gate. "Want to grab a Coke? I work weekends at the cafe over there. It's not far—think I can make it."

A knot forms in my stomach at the prospect of a

slow walk. I tuck my skateboard under one arm and quell the desire to burn off my simmering energy. I force a smile. "Sure, sounds good."

At the kerbside, I shuffle my feet and try to ignore the deep unease enveloping me. It's like knowing I'm about to bail but being helpless to avoid it.

Noa's head droops and he slumps forward on his crutches.

I touch his arm. "Are you alright?" Bad vibes seem to be infecting both of us.

"The cast's heavy and these things kill my arms." He raises a crutch off the ground.

A stab of guilt momentarily distracts me from the urge to move. Knowing his suffering is my fault isn't getting any easier to handle.

A decent gap in traffic appears and I run to the middle of the road to wait for Noa. A faint chemical odour drifts across and I straighten up. *Please no, not here.* Fear immobilises me and my feet stick onto the white line. The skull ring appears. Its glaring ruby eyes and shining silver bear down on me. Muffled shouting filters through to me but doesn't make any sense. The chemical smell burns my throat and breathing is like sucking air in through a straw. Car wheels skid against asphalt and gravel raps against my legs followed by the blast of a car horn. Shouting jolts me.

Noa grabs my arm and propels me forward. "Marvel, Marvel! Quick, get across."

I crumple onto pavement and squeeze my fingers into the firm brown flesh of Noa's arm, desperate to connect with something tangible, something I can trust.

He sits beside me. "That was way different from the hospital one." His eyes dart to the road, then back to my face. "You almost got run over. I stuck my crutch out just in time."

I lift my hand off his arm and cover my hot cheeks with my palms. "I should go. All I've done is bring you bad luck." I'll take the bullying over this vision anytime. I feel like a kid learning to skate: rolling aimlessly across the base of the skate bowl, tears of frustration welling up at my lack of control, doubting I'll ever understand how it works.

"Trust me, I know what bad luck is." Noa's voice is flat.

I uncover my face.

Noa stares past me and his eyes glaze with sadness. He shakes his head. "Come on." He hauls himself to standing and points a crutch towards the cafe.

I grasp onto one of his crutches and heave myself up, then wait for him to set off.

Noa's right. As a measure of bad luck, losing your dad is off the scale.

The cafe is quiet and smells of boiled milk. I inhale a ragged breath and take a long sip of Coke. The cool syrupy liquid soothes my dry throat and replenishes my energy. My thoughts clear and the significance of what just happened sinks in. Did this vision come to finish me off? Maybe Noa's fall was the last straw, exhausting the last drops of patience the psychic world had in me. Doubt they've ever chosen a messenger as crap as me before.

Noa's Coke glass is empty and he hasn't said a word. His strong, silent presence feels like a forcefield around me. It crosses my mind that if spirits were intent on taking me out, then why was Noa there to save me?

I meet his eyes and hesitate. I'm not sure whether I can tell him the truth about this vision. It feels like I'm revealing all the ugly parts of me that I prefer to hide, like my jagged scars and the dent in my thigh muscle from when I skated into an outdoor table. But I get the impression Noa isn't the kind of person who rushes to judge. I inhale. "This vision's not like the others. It's terrifying." I battle my emotions. "It's like …" I clasp my shaking hands together, "it's possessing me."

Noa takes my hands in his. "What do you see?"

"A skull ring on a finger."

"Whose finger?" His voice is calm and in his gentle grip my trembling hands slow.

"All I see is a finger."

He smiles. "Sounds like something out of the *X-Files*."

I sigh, give a weak smile back. "I wish it was off the TV." I level with him and take a deep breath in. "Do you think I'm crazy?"

He grins. "Only when you legged it into the middle of the road without me."

I look down and know my cheeks are reddening again.

Noa phones a cab. He says they're free for a few weeks to help him get to and from school. It turns out his house isn't far from mine.

He waves to the taxi parked outside and turns to me. "Want a lift?"

"I'd love one, thanks." I long to return home to skate my favourite streets and shore up some defence against the vision recurring.

The driver stops outside a small brick house with a red tiled roof. There's a mini soccer net on the front lawn and a potholed driveway slopes up one side of the house.

I clamber out, then reach back into the car and hand Noa his crutches.

By the front door of the house is an old bookshelf crammed with shoes. There's so many, they spill out onto the doorstep, creating a mountain of colour and tangled laces. Small faces appear at the window, springing into view one after another, their breath steaming up the glass. Five children beam down at me, their hands waving and tapping on the window.

"Here's the welcome party. Bet they're wondering where I've been." Noa shuffles along the seat to the car door and levers himself out, then pulls silly faces at the children.

"Do you want to come in for a bit?" His voice is hopeful.

The pull to skate is strong. My fear of this inscrutable vision returning clouds everything. I look into Noa's soft brown eyes and wish I could say yes. I shake my head and start to speak, but my voice is drowned out by a stampede of children rushing out of the house towards me. Tiny hands grip mine and someone tugs my T-shirt, dragging me up the driveway. The children surround me, their wide eyes darting from me to Noa as if their big brother hanging out with a girl is front page news.

"What's your name?" asks a young boy.

"Marvel."

"That's a funny name," says his sister. "Are you Noa's girlfriend?"

"What?" I yank my hands free. "No."

"Are you in the friend zone?" says another boy, laughing.

"I think you should get married," says the older sister. "Can I be the flower girl?"

"*I* want to be the flower girl," says the smallest girl, elbowing her sister in the ribs.

"Easy now, you lot." He sends me an apologetic look, then turns to the children. "Marvel, this is, Luisa, Isaia, Tavita and the youngest little monkey …" he ruffles the hair of the smallest child, "is Teuila."

Teuila grabs my hand and holds it tight. "Come on, Marvel."

I stumble up the drive, torn from the long stretch

of smooth pavement behind me. I glance back and into Noa's sparkling eyes. "Alright. I'll stay for twenty minutes, max."

Inside, the smell of jasmine reminds me of Sadie's garden and the day I spent hours cutting her jasmine plant back, its milky sap sticking to my fingers, hindering my progress.

A tall woman with jet black hair pulled tight off her forehead stands at the kitchen door. She bats the air with the back of her palms, ushering the kids away.

The children scurry off, feet pattering along the wooden floor. Doors crash shut behind them.

"Welcome. I'm Emmeline, Noa's mother." She draws herself up and rolls her shoulders back.

I hold her gaze and force my voice to stay strong. "I'm Marvella, but everyone calls me Marvel. Good to meet you."

She steps back and looks me up and down. "Marvella is much nicer."

I grimace and immediately regret giving her my full name; only Sadie calls me Marvella.

Her face lights up. "You're the girl who tended his broken ankle. Thank you. The bone's healing well. All those metal plates and screws—the X-rays were a sight to behold."

I inhale sharply and glance across to Noa. "Oh."

Emmeline reaches over to the wall and unhooks her coat. "It wasn't your fault, sweetheart."

Noa nudges me and lifts a finger to his lips.

I tilt up my chin. *Don't worry, Noa, I won't say anything.*

Emmeline turns around and pulls on a beige trenchcoat. She shoots Noa a reproachful look. "He needs to watch where he's going and stop wearing those stupid headphones." She brushes down her coat and buckles up the belt. "I'm off to work. Hope to see you again, Marvel. God bless."

"Yes. Err, thanks." I let out a long breath.

Noa peers into the kitchen. "Just need to do the rice and school lunches?"

"Get Luisa to help." Emmeline stops. She raises her eyes to a plain wooden crucifix above the front door and makes the sign of the cross. The door clicks shut behind her.

Noa gives a tight smile and tilts his head towards the back of the house. "Want to see my studio?"

I look down the hallway and tally up the doors: two bedrooms, bathroom, lounge. "Where is it?"

Noa laughs. "It's outside—there's no space or peace in here."

"Right." I check my watch; ten minutes gone already.

Through fading light, I traipse over broken paving stones and follow Noa to the garden shed. The lower half is hidden by long grass and weeds. The only window is cracked, held in place by brown parcel tape.

Noa leans against the warped door and opens the padlock. "I should've given you a heads up—Mum believes anything supernatural is black magic, so best not to mention your visions."

I've had this same opinion thrown at me many times, but coming from Noa, the words shatter me. It's like a boulder rolling across the path and separating us. "My grandmother, Sadie is a Catholic. She read palms at the church fair for years and no one complained."

Noa sighs. "Sorry, that's just how she is. No point discussing it." He turns back to the door and shoves it open.

I pause on the threshold with one hand against the door. Being psychic isn't something I chose. It's part of who I am and believe me, not a day goes by when I don't question why on earth I inherited this so-called Gift.

Inside, it smells of turps and I wedge the door ajar to allow fresh air in. The floor is spongy under my feet like a wrecked skateboard deck. Paintbrushes and tubes of acrylic paint are neatly arranged on a fold-out table next to an easel. A bare light bulb dangles from the apex of the roof. Its cable has split, revealing coloured wires.

Noa sits on a stool by the easel. Its vinyl cover is coming away at the edges. "Cool studio, isn't it?" He sounds proud.

"It's great." I force my voice to lift.

The pencil sketch pinned to the easel shows a beautifully painted purple hibiscus flower. Next to it is a sketch of a girl with long dark hair.

I tense; she looks like me. I stare at the picture, then slowly shift my gaze to Noa.

He screws on the lid of a paint tube and drops it into a cardboard box on the floor.

I feel self-conscious and awkward, like how I used to in my early days of skating, when I was the only girl at the skate park and the boys kept staring at me.

Noa locks eyes with me and I feel my cheeks redden.

Scrambling for words, I splutter out the first thought that surfaces. "Mum's an artist. I think you'd like her stuff. Come over this weekend if you like?" *Why did I say that? What if he gets the wrong impression?*

"Sure. I'll come over after work tomorrow. They're going to sort something out even though I'm on crutches—I need the cash."

I hold open the door for Noa. My heart is heavy and confused. There's enough unanswered questions floating around without me adding more. I stare at his back and listen to the click of his crutches against the garden path. No way can I leave here without knowing how he feels.

Noa zigzags down his driveway to avoid the potholes and stands beside me on the pavement.

I drop my skateboard onto concrete and face him.

"Noa. We're just friends, right?" I hold my breath.

Noa steps back. "Yeah. Course. A friend's what you need most, isn't it?"

My breath rushes out. "Err, you're kind of my only friend." I look down. He's probably thinking I'm such a sad-sack.

"Well then, I'm the lucky one."

I glance up and smile. A weight lifts off me.

His eyes plead. "If anything bad happens or if you need help, call me. Anytime."

His kind offer makes me too emotional to speak. I gaze out into the dusk and try to pull myself together. "I'll be fine."

"You weren't fine before."

I turn around, but avoid his eyes. "No."

A text message pings. I slide my phone out of my back pocket. It's a reminder about my hair appointment with Vince. Unease creeps over me and a surge of anxiety rises up in my chest. *Am I really going to save him? How?*

Noa's voice fills with concern. "Everything alright?"

I force a smile. "Yeah. It's nothing." I push off and raise my voice over the rumbling wheels beneath me. "See you Saturday."

I glance back to Noa. He looks worried.

My lip quivers and tears fill my eyes, all my pent-up emotion finally breaking free and blurring the path ahead.

CHAPTER FOUR

I release the glass salon door and feel a waft of air against my legs. The atmosphere inside the white cubic space of Bad Hair Daze reminds me of when my cat died and no one wanted to tell me. The tension is aggravated by harsh electronic music pumping in the background. My heart thumps hard and fast, mimicking the beat of the music. I'm on strange turf here, like visiting a small town skate park and trying to blend in with the locals. I stand by the empty reception desk and nibble my nails. The urge to walk back out is hard to resist. A black leather couch and two potted tropical palms, their frond tips brownish-yellow, form an L-shape in front of the reception desk. Beyond them, a sea of grey concrete floor butts up to a wall of mirrors where three stylists snip hair. I take a deep breath and tell myself to stay; I'm here for more than just a haircut.

I prop my skateboard against the block wall behind the couch, then slide onto smooth leather cushions.

The desire to leg it comes over me again and I press my feet to the floor.

One of the stylists walks over. His shoulders hunch up to his ears and black jeans hang off his hips. He stretches out a limp bony hand.

"Hi, Marvel. I'm Vince." He forces a smile. "You're all grown up." Skin puckers around his mouth and the whites of his eyes are tracked with veins.

I shake his clammy hand. "Hi." His breath smells like Dad's when he's got a hangover—sour, like poison's being flushed out. His clothes reek of cigarettes. Whatever's gone down since I was a kid doesn't seem to have done him much good.

Vince combs his fingers through my hair, stopping frequently to untangle knots. His hands shake and he clutches them together so tightly his fingertips turn white. Hopefully I'll make it out of here with both ears intact. Swirly lettering's tattooed up his left forearm and I squint to read it: *Shirley*. His mum's name. Sadness sweeps over me. I think he was only five when she died.

He mutters into my ear, "Your hair's a shambles. Been cutting it yourself?"

"Err, yep. Sorry."

He tilts his chin up and down. "It's okay, you're in good hands. I'll work my Vince magic on you." His voice is a monotone, like all the joy's been wrung out.

I look into the reflection of his hollow eyes. "I just want a trim and—" I clamp my mouth shut and look away. The need to discover how I'm supposed to help him burns inside me.

He glances at me. "I'll tidy the ends. Don't panic."

I think about how I can bring it up without sounding like a fairy tale knight galloping towards him on a white horse.

"When did you last see Sadie?" I try to sound casual.

"I did her hair a few weeks ago. Why?"

I meet his eyes in the mirror. "Did she say anything about *me*?"

He stops cutting my hair and shoots me a confused look. "She said you'd be coming in."

Pride wells up inside me and I smile. "Well, she predicts I'm going to help you." I don't say "save", that sounds way too dramatic, like a cheesy Hollywood movie.

Vince stiffens. "It's good to see you, Marvel, but I don't need your help." His voice is robotic and his words are like an elbow jutting into my guts.

I sink my head.

"Has Sadie been reading your palm?" Vince's contemptuous tone strikes another blow to my insides.

"So, palm-reading and psychic stuff aren't your thing?" I pause. "But, wasn't your mum, Shirley, a psychic? Sadie says she recorded all she saw in journals."

"So I hear." He hesitates. "Keep meaning to

get those journals from Sadie." He grimaces. "Not because of their content—I don't give a crap about that." He hesitates and his lower lip trembles. "I just want something that was hers." His eyes lower and his arms flop to his sides. "I suppose fetching me those would be some help."

Did everything happen too young for Vince? Losing his mum, then his dad dying when he was nineteen. Awarded Hairdresser of the Year at only twenty-one. A life of massive highs and lows, like being strapped into a roller-coaster you can't get off.

I look at Vince's sad, weary face in the mirror and sympathy wells up. My resolve to help him hasn't waned, and whether he thinks he needs my help or not, it's fated. Retrieving Shirley's journals for him is better than nothing, but since when did a stash of journals save anyone?

Vince raises a section of my hair between his fingers. His face contorts with the effort of lifting the scissors and slicing across the band of hair. I feel tired just watching him.

He takes a deep breath. "So, what do you do outside school?"

"I skate, listen to music, deal with whatever the psychic world throws at me," I say, deadpan.

Vince looks at me with a puzzled expression. "I catch your dad's radio show sometimes. He plays some great tunes." He has a distant look in his eyes. "I tried to visit you so many times when you were a kid."

An idea sparks. "Come over sometime. I'm sure I can persuade Dad."

Vince shakes his head and looks down. "Sadie already tried. Your dad won't budge. He has his reasons, but—"

"What reasons?" I straighten up.

Vince stops cutting. "The money."

"What money?"

Vince's eyes narrow.

"You're family. I won't take sides." My voice is firm.

He sighs and his shoulders sag forward like he's shrinking in on himself. "A few years ago, my partner Grant asked Sadie to invest in his magazine. He can't repay her—the magazine's struggling." His voice drops to a whisper. "Grant says it's all my fault."

Vague memories return. Fierce whispers between Dad and Sadie when they thought I couldn't hear. "Why's it your fault?"

He pushes back his greasy fringe. "*Edge* magazine did well at first. I styled the photo shoots and advertising rolled in. Other magazines even tried to headhunt me. But, it all got a bit much." He pauses, inhales. "Grant made me use designers I didn't even like, took over—" He swallows hard, his Adam's apple pokes out like a jabbing finger.

"So, you left and started here?"

"Yeah. Been dining out on that Hairdresser of the Year award for a while now." He smiles weakly.

Questions fizz in my mind, surfacing one after the

other, each one more pressing than the last. How am I supposed to help? I can't save a magazine.

Vince untangles the hairdryer cord and reaches for a brush. He mutters something about hair product, then there's no sound, just his lips moving.

Oh, no, not in here. I screw up my eyes and brace myself. The silver skull ring appears on a stubby finger and swings in an arc like a skater on a halfpipe. The chemical smell and the motion of the ring make me nauseous and I swallow down bitter saliva. Breathing in tightens my throat and my heart pounds, sending another wave of panic through me.

The vision releases me from its grip and I pitch forwards, gasping for air.

Vince presses a cold flannel to my forehead. "You nearly fainted." He shouts to a junior to fetch a glass of water.

I push the flannel away. "I'm alright." I fight back tears. *What is this vision telling me?*

I swivel around and search Vince's hands for rings, then breathe a sigh of relief. At least I can rule him out. I gulp back water so fast, it spills down my front. I tug apart the gown's press studs and let it slip from my shoulders.

Vince plugs in a hairdryer. "I'll just finish off."

I stand up and eye the door. "It can air dry. I need to get out of here." I stride across the room and grab my skateboard. The board's plywood curves mould into the crook of my arm like the missing piece of a jigsaw. A whiff of chemical drifts from the open storeroom door. I stop. It's the smell from the vision: ammonia from hair dye. I narrow my eyes; the smell is in *here*.

Vince's voice is at my shoulder, desperate. "Please keep in touch, promise me."

My sweaty hand slides off the door handle. "Yes, course I will."

His eyes light up.

"Look, I'm sorry about rushing off. The psychic world's doing my head in." I force a smile and try to give the impression that this isn't a big deal.

Vince's brow furrows. "Get yourself a snack or something, can't have you fainting like that again."

I sigh. My gaze latches onto the clock above the door. Its hands stopped at 9.30—my appointment time.

"What a piece of crap. I only just changed the batteries," says Vince.

I shake my head. There's no point even trying to explain about clocks. "See you soon. I'll get your mum's stuff." I push open the door. Fresh air cools my cheek and I take a deep breath.

My legs itch to move but there's nowhere safe to skate. The pavement's crowded with Saturday shoppers and Ponsonby Road's a deathtrap of speeding SUVs. People mill around aimlessly and a couple next to me gawp into the window of a fancy, overpriced cake shop.

I run; weave my way through throngs of people, ducking and twisting to avoid collision. My legs brush against paper shopping bags and a dog lead almost trips me over—I right myself, then get a blast of coffee aroma. Laughter and music bursts from shop fronts and a bright window display dazzles me. It's all too much and I long for quieter suburban streets. I push myself to keep going even though my burning legs and aching chest scream at me to rest. I'm heading the opposite way from the bus stop on purpose, because by the time I board that bus I must be exhausted. The last thing I need is the skull ring making an appearance on the Auckland Inner Link.

◆

I choose a seat at the back of the bus where there's less chance of anyone noticing if I act strange. The bus trundles along Ponsonby Road, passing designer shops, bars and restaurants. They blur into insignificance as my mind tries to process what happened in the salon. I clutch my head in my hands and damp hair swings down, forming a curtain across my face. Tears of bitter disappointment stream down my cheeks. Sadie's prediction gave me purpose and hope. I dread telling her the bad news: she was wrong and I'm not going to save Vince after all. Fetching him Aunt Shirley's stuff and talking to Dad about visiting is some consolation, I suppose, especially considering the miserable state Vince was in. But, helping isn't in the same league as saving.

I close my eyes and relive the embarrassment I felt at the vision coming back. What a coincidence the smell was.

A text message beeps. It's Noa asking what time he should come over later. A warm feeling eases my sadness. I text him back and send a happy face emoji, even though I feel anything but.

As the bus turns a corner, I see the playground vision again. Two giggling boys having fun on the swings and across from them a kid flies down a slide, then lands shrieking on soft bark. The vision pans out to rows of new builds: white rendered terraces with sections of timber cladding and tiny front yards. I've no idea where it is, there's no place like that around here.

I count the stops to home, not far now. I wipe my face with my T-shirt sleeve and summon the courage to tell Sadie that her prediction is seriously out of whack.

CHAPTER FIVE

My freshly washed hair smells of mandarin-scented shampoo mixed with diesel fumes. I run up the hill and straight to Sadie's.

"Hi," I say breathlessly.

Sadie's got her key in the door. She turns to me. "Oh, hello Marvella. Good you caught me, I'm just back from the hospital, my friend's not got long."

All Sadie's friends seem to be dying, she'll have none left soon.

She smiles. "At least that's one thing Catholics and psychics have in common, the belief that death isn't the end."

I think of Emmeline; not so sure she'd agree with that.

Sadie ushers me inside. "Quick sandwich?"

"Perfect." I follow her to the kitchen. I'm so close behind, my trainers catch her shoe heels.

"I had my hair cut."

She swivels around from the kitchen bench.

"Wonderful." She looks out of the French doors leading to the garden. "And how was Vince?"

"A mess. Depressed. Guilty about you losing that money." I hesitate and take a deep breath. "I'm not going to save him, Sadie. All he wants is Shirley's stuff and to fix the rift with Dad."

"Mmm, not a happy chappie is he?" Sadie passes me a sandwich on a pale green hexagonal-shaped plate. She's cut my sandwich into quarters and hers in half. At least she's stopped cutting the crusts off mine.

I bite into the soft white bread, but don't register its taste.

Sadie stares at the wall, then shakes her shoulders as if disengaging from her thoughts. "It was a risky investment, but I wanted to help Vince and Grant out. The other guy, what's his name? Oh, yes, Alex someone or other. He invested a lot more—dread to think how much." Sadie's gaze shifts to the floor. "I promised Shirley I'd always look after him." She meets my eyes. "Remember when Uncle William, Vince's dad, died?"

I nod, remembering I got a day off from intermediate school for the funeral.

Sadie's voice hardens. "Well, I'm afraid after that, Vince hit the drink. It was a miracle he got that hairdresser award. Imagine how good he'd have been sober." She pauses. "Then, he met Grant who seemed nice at first …"

I look at Sadie and sigh. Did she even hear what I said about not saving Vince?

"I'm going to talk to Dad about his grudge."

"Well, good luck with that," says Sadie with a light laugh.

Irritation rises up. "You predicted I'm going to help him, so I will—it's important to me."

Sadie straightens up. "Not help, *save*. Shirley predicted it before she died."

I push my plate across the table. "But I wasn't even born then."

Sadie's eyes glaze over and she tugs at the chain of pearls around her neck. "The day before Shirley passed, she told me Simon's teenage daughter would save Vince." She dabs the corner of her eyes with a tissue.

"But how and from what?" I stare at Sadie's blank face.

She shrugs. "I wouldn't worry too much about the ins and outs. It'll become obvious at some point." Sadie's gaze lifts to the ceiling, like she's acknowledging a higher power. She looks at me. "Be patient and don't forget—" she reaches for my hands, "I'm always here for you."

I jerk my hands away. I'm not a little girl anymore. "Where's Shirley's stuff?"

Sadie carries the plates over to the sink. "Oh, yes, he keeps going on about that box. It's in the attic. I'm far too old to be going up ladders." She rinses two plates and stacks them in the dishwasher.

"I'll go up, then."

"Yes, okay. You'll need to fetch your dad's stepladder."

I pull Sadie's front door shut and sit on the steps outside her house to gather my thoughts. The sky has clouded over and a cool breeze catches my hair and I shiver. I wrap my arms around myself to keep warm and let the bracing air focus my thinking. My eyes lock onto the perfectly straight box hedge and I sigh. Nothing in the natural world is straight; why do humans have to mess with everything? Shirley's deathbed prediction is all very well, but Vince doesn't believe in psychics, even when that psychic is his own mother. That's the problem with predictions; I'm only the messenger. Success hinges on the belief system of the person I'm trying to help. Vince is family, he's blood, and if the least I can do is brave Sadie's attic and fish out Shirley's box of belongings, well, it's better than nothing. And as for fixing his grudge with Dad; I'll save that battle for later. Don't get me wrong, I'd love to save Vince, but human nature is a force I can't fight.

I stand up and try to remember where I last saw Dad's stepladder.

◆

Well, that was a mission. I drop the cardboard box onto my bedroom carpet and shove it against the wall. Sadie's attic was an assault course of bulging bin bags, boxes and piles of books. I almost put my foot through the ceiling trying to hold the torch while rummaging around for Shirley's stuff. Sadie's vague directions made me want to scream; "Somewhere at the back" doesn't exactly narrow down the search when the entire roof space is full of crap. Anyway, it's good I found it and worth getting covered in spider webs and dust for the opportunity to cheer up Vince.

My room's stuffy and I'm sweating from the effort of lugging the box and stepladder back home. I open the window too far and lose my grip on the latch. A sudden gust of wind slams the window frame back against the house. A crack like a flash of lightning ruptures the glass. The ammonia smell returns. I jump onto the bed and pull my knees to my chest, readying myself for the onslaught.

I take short, shallow breaths. "Stay calm, Marvel, it'll pass," I whisper. This time the vision's different. Two arms swing in a semi-circle, but they're two *left* arms. It's not the skull ring that dominates this vision but the other arm, the one with swirly lettering tattooed up the forearm, spelling the name *Shirley*. I gasp. *It's Vince's arm.*

Voices carry from the lounge. A gentle knock on my door.

"Noa's here, can I send him in?" says Mum.

"Can you show him your art? I'm just getting changed, won't be a minute." I keep my voice calm even though my head's bursting.

I scoop up dirty clothes from the carpet and chuck them in a pile behind my bed. I sit on the bed and try to compose myself, but questions erupt inside my head like fizz in a shaken bottle of lemonade, pressure building up with no way out. Rational thought is impossible. This room is stifling and I lunge for the door handle.

In the lounge, Noa gives me a wave and smiles. His gaze shifts back to Mum's large abstract painting and he says it reminds him of a painting by Georgia O'Keefe.

Mum's art is part of the wallpaper. It's strange to see Noa so intent on the painting's waves of colour and the unearthly shapes that float across it.

Mum blushes. "I love her work. I'm very flattered, but my own pales in comparison. What do you paint?"

"Portraits. After my dad died I'd spend days at the art gallery staring at the Goldies and Lindauers." He looks down. "It helped me. I liked how the essence of a person could be captured in such a powerful way."

Mum sighs. "That's the beauty of representational art. I like the freedom of abstraction, how it's open to interpretation, the way it transports the viewer into a different world. Personally, Marvel's experiences with the spiritual plane have been a huge influence."

Thoughts about the vision ping inside my brain like popping candy, distracting me from Mum and Noa's conversation.

Mum looks over at me. "Marvel's coming, you can go with her."

I frown. "Go where?"

Mum shakes her head and the long copper shards dangling from her ears sway. "My art exhibition next Friday, remember?"

"Oh, yes. Sorry, I forgot." It comes out a bit flat. Mum's art show is not exactly at the forefront of my mind right now.

Noa looks from me to Mum and there's an awkward silence.

"I'd better get back to work. Great to meet you, Noa. I'm glad the leg's healing and maybe see you tomorrow with your portfolio?"

"That'd be awesome. Thanks, Julia."

Mum wanders back to her studio down the hall. Her floaty top wafts around her slim frame and her bracelets chime together. A flowery scent lingers in the lounge.

"What's the matter?" he says as soon as Mum is out of earshot.

I beckon him into my room and point to the cracked window.

His eyes widen and he touches the crack in the glass. "A vision did that?"

"Yep." I meet his eyes. "I need to get out of here." My hands shake and I feel faint. I think the shock is kicking in, and the realisation that the smell in the hairdresser's was no coincidence.

Noa nods and links my arm.

My legs wobble and I wait a few seconds before I trust my feet can hold me.

Noa reaches over and closes the window. "Right,

let's get you some fresh air." He tilts his head towards the door.

The cool air perks me up. I glance at Noa sidelong and wonder how he learnt to read me so easily. I didn't need to explain how the window cracked. Nothing's prepared me for a vision like this, one that almost suffocates me to get its message across.

Sadie's always been my confidant but, at seventeen and a half, it's pretty lame running to my grandma every time I'm worried. I don't really want to tell Noa, either, but he's seen what this vision does to me, how helpless and vulnerable it makes me. I'm scared, and to be honest, I'm not brave enough to go it alone. If anything bad happens to me, at least Noa will know what I was going through.

Noa's breathing grows more laboured.

"Can you make it to the park?" My special place isn't far, maybe a hundred metres on the flat.

"I think so, if I take it slow." Noa propels himself forwards and prods the pedestrian crossing button with the end of one crutch.

I lead Noa away from the path, through a copse of trees and down an overgrown grassy slope to a wooden bench.

Noa sits down and kicks off his trainers, letting them roll into the long grass below. "How did you find this spot?" Sweat along his hairline sticks down his curls.

"I bailed on the corner and my board flew through the trees."

Noa laughs. "I guessed it would be something dramatic."

I nudge him in the ribs. Usually, drama chooses me, not the other way round.

A bird flits around in the branches of a tree and rustles the leaves. The daylight is fading and it's colder now. I fold my arms against my chest, wishing I'd brought my hoody. Despite being cold, this place is my sanctuary and for the first time since I saw Vince's tattoo and my window broke, I feel ready to talk about what happened. "I saw my cousin Vince's arm in the vision."

Noa pulls a bottle of supermarket-brand fizzy drink out of his backpack and twists off the cap. "The cousin you're meant to be saving?" He takes a swig, then offers it to me.

I take a sip and wince. The drink has the sickly aftertaste of artificial sweetener. "Yes. There were two left arms, but it wasn't Vince wearing the ring." I turn to him and see confusion in his eyes. "I know. It's messing with my head, too."

"Right." Noa blows air out and his eyes search mine. "Is that good or bad news for Vince?"

"I'm pretty sure it's bad. Everything about this vision is bad."

"What are you going to do?"

"Warn Vince. I think that's what I'm meant to do."

Maybe the vision will stop bugging me once I do what it wants?

I tell Noa about retrieving Shirley's box and how I plan on returning it to Vince.

Noa hesitates, then turns to me, his face serious. "I know you're scared. I would be."

My cheeks burn hot. Emotional honesty isn't something I'm used to expressing. I've always been the girl who puts on a brave face, like with the bullies from my old school or the time I ripped my knee to shreds at the skate park and told the other skaters I was fine. Anything to avoid attracting attention.

"I *am* scared. And it's worse when your own family's involved."

"Families are complicated." Noa hesitates and his gaze drifts to the trees.

I wonder if he's referring to his mother.

He places his hand on top of mine. "Call me anytime. Don't deal with all this on your own."

I sigh. "I'll try."

Noa drains the bottle of drink. "I better get going. I'll see you tomorrow; your mum's helping me with my art school portfolio."

"Okay. I might go for a skate, try and keep the spirits away." The sun's dipping behind trees and I'll need to get a move on before it grows dark.

"Does it work?" His voice is matter of fact. It amazes me how well he's adjusting to my freakish world.

"Intense exercise blocks them. But sometimes they still get through."

"Does the skull ring vision get through?"

A shiver goes through me and I think of Vince, knowing more misfortune is heading his way. "Yeah. That one's a whole other level."

I walk with him back to the road and help him into the taxi.

Responsibility weighs heavily upon me. I search up Vince's hair salon on my phone. It re-opens on Tuesday. I swallow. That's ample time to tackle the other issue I keep putting off: the rift between Dad and Vince.

CHAPTER SIX

I move Shirley's box to the hallway and push it into the alcove where the coats hang. My lower legs are covered in bruises from tripping over it, a side effect of having the world's tiniest bedroom.

Dad reaches over my shoulder to grab his coat. He's wearing his ultra embarrassing Iron Maiden T-shirt; grotesque and cheesy in equal measure. His foot kicks against the box, which Sadie labelled in thick black Sharpie: *Shirley's Journals*. He glares at me. "Shirley? What are you doing with this?"

"Vince wants it." I hesitate. "I wanted to talk to you about him."

He pulls on his battered denim jacket. "Don't invite him round here." He looks in the mirror and slicks back his grey hair.

"Why not?"

Dad turns to me. "I can't stop *you* seeing him. Just avoid him drunk, he's not pretty and if he offers you a pipe, don't smoke it." He checks his watch and taps on the glass. "Christ, Marvel, you and the bloody time. I'm late."

"Dad, you didn't answer my—" The door crashes shut and he's off to his radio show.

My face burns with frustration. I need answers.

I bowl into Mum's studio, flinging the door with such force that the handle hits the wall and a chunk of white plaster falls to the floor. "Why did Dad fall out with Vince?"

Mum startles and drops her paintbrush onto the ledge below her easel. "Marvel!" Her blue eyes blaze.

I clench my hands. "Dad won't tell me. He's my cousin and I have a right to know."

Mum sighs. She tucks a loose strand of blonde hair behind her ear. "Okay. But yelling and barging in on me isn't going to get you very far."

My hands go to my face. I mumble through the gaps in my fingers, "Sorry. I just need to know." I almost tell her about the vision to justify my meltdown, but stop myself. I'm too old to be crying to my mother.

I stand at her side. A slash of yellow paint slants across the lower part of the canvas from where the paintbrush fell and my heart sinks. "I'm really sorry, Mum."

"Easily fixed." Mum's hand sweeps across the line turning it white and it disappears into the background. She fixes her gaze on me. "Why the sudden interest in Vince?"

I pause. "He's the nearest I've got to a brother." If I can manage to convince Mum without mentioning either the vision or Sadie's prediction, it will save her a lot of worry.

"You know how stubborn your father is. I think he'd like to see Vince but grudges fester."

"What started it?"

Mum shakes her head. "Vince visited a lot when you were little. He's a good person, but his drinking got bad. One day he was so drunk he knocked you over and hurt you. Your father—"

I interrupt. She doesn't need to tell me the details. I know Dad would've lost the plot. "Is the money part of it, too?"

She hesitates. "Oh. Vince told you?"

I nod.

"Yes. Sadie only told us after she'd sent the money. And Grant …" Her gaze drifts to the floor.

"What about him?"

Mum shudders. "He cares for no one but himself." She takes my hand. "Get to know Vince on your own terms. Keep your father out of it."

I sigh. At least I can tell Vince I tried.

Mum's eyes bore into me. "You seem on edge lately. Has something happened?"

I squirm and say the first thing that comes into my head. "My bedroom window cracked. It shook me up."

"Cracked how? A supernatural force?" Her voice lifts.

"No, the wind caught it. Good old Mother Nature." I force a smile.

"Okay. I'll take a look later." She looks doubtful. Reassurance and a sympathetic ear used to be all I needed when I was younger, but that's not going to help me now.

A text comes in. I look at Mum. "Noa's on his way over."

◆

Mum and Noa are engrossed in the world of art again, discussing their favourite hues of colour. Noa favours Ultramarine Blue, Lemon Yellow and Cadmium Red. He mentions he's thinking of giving abstraction a try.

Mum looks pleased. "Go for it. Channel your grief through a different style. I'm sure it'll help."

I'm redundant, having nothing meaningful to contribute to the discussion. Wish I'd listened when Mum used to discuss her art, but it always sounded so airy-fairy and it annoys me that she creates these beautiful pictures about the world I live in, when the reality is, there is nothing remotely beautiful about being psychic.

Piles of Noa's drawings cover the dining table and I flick through them, feeling relieved he chose to paint portraits. At least there are no hidden messages or profound meanings within his kind of art.

Mum deliberates for ages over every picture, scrutinising each one up close and deciding whether it warrants a place in Noa's portfolio.

I sip my third cup of tea and pretend to look interested. All I can think about is Vince and what the vision may signify.

Dad walks in with a jubilant look on his face. "Well, that's the cobwebs blown off the airwaves for another week. Oh, hello," he says, noticing Noa.

"Noa, this is my dad, Simon."

Noa sticks out his hand. His gaze shifts to Dad's T-shirt. "Cool shirt."

"Marvel's a huge fan," says Dad, winding me up.

I roll my eyes. "Yeah, right."

"I'm more of a hip hop man myself." Noa grins. "They play your radio show in the cafe where I work. It's pretty loud. Clears a few tables."

Dad looks proud. "I take no prisoners."

Grey areas don't exist for Dad. He doesn't believe in a middle ground and while this makes him good at writing opinion pieces, the flip side is he's not easily persuaded to change his mind.

Dad holds up a sheet of Noa's art. "Nice. You helping him, Julia?"

"Yes. Noa's applying to study Fine Art at Whitecliffe College." She squints at a picture. "It's tough to narrow it down. Your work is excellent."

Dad's face lights up. "Ah, you're the guy who got hurt."

"Yep." Noa looks embarrassed.

I shift in my chair.

Dad looks at me and shakes his head. "What a

dilemma that was. Risk more bullying by warning you or keep quiet and watch the carnage unfold."

Noa shoots me a sympathetic glance. "Yeah, it's even worse when they keep coming back and she can't breathe."

Dad turns to me, his voice sharp. "What the hell? Which vision keeps coming back?"

Here we go. I take a slow, deep breath. "The one involving Vince."

Mum lays down the picture she's holding.

Noa mouths the word, *sorry*.

"It's okay," I whisper. He wasn't to know Mum and Dad were in the dark.

I play down the part about not being able to breathe and miss out the bit where I almost got run over. If I told them about every danger I encountered, including all the touch-and-go skateboard jumps, such as the time I ollied down the steps near the art gallery convinced I was going to die, they'd be nervous wrecks. Were my previous dices with death preparing me for this? Well, even if the spirit world considers I'm worthy of the challenge, it doesn't mean I'm not bricking myself.

Dad passes round steaming mugs of tea. He takes a sip, then looks at me. "You're a lot like Shirley. I just wish you hadn't inherited my sister's psychic ability. It blighted her life and now it's doing the same to yours, dragging you into Vince's tawdry life. I don't like it one little bit." He thumps his mug down and tea slops onto the coaster.

I tear off a sliver of thumbnail with my teeth. "I don't get a choice. He's your nephew, Dad. We're the only family he has left and he needs us." I pause. "I'm going to warn him about the vision when I give him the box."

"Grant probably wants to check there's nothing in that box worth selling." Dad spits out his words.

"Sadie says it's just her journals and old photos." A thought comes to me. "You know Vince listens to your show?"

Dad mumbles, "As do most millennials in this city."

I give up.

Noa sends me a feeble smile.

"Let your father mull it over. He needs to let thoughts percolate." Mum reaches across and pats my arm. Her hand is covered in dots of yellow paint.

Dad grunts and takes another sip of tea.

Mum picks up a sketch and places it on a second, smaller pile. "Okay, Noa. This one's a definite."

"You reckon? I wasn't sure about that portrait of Dad." He looks from Dad to me and sadness flickers across his face.

I smell ammonia. "Noa," I shout and grip the chair arms tight. The furniture and art on the walls blur into amorphous shapes. Mum, Dad and Noa transform into shadows. They remind me of the ghost I sometimes see lurking by the skatepark toilets. Panic engulfs me. *Are they dead?* I reach a shaky hand towards them and it knocks against something solid. The vision of two arms appears, Vince's tattoo on one, the skull ring on the other. Above them, a pink neon sign glows against a black wall. It spells the word *Flava*.

I take a deep breath and the room comes back into focus. *Oh god, no.* My mug of tea is on its side and beige liquid runs in rivulets over the dining table, soaking into Noa's art.

Dad's face is deathly white.

Mum races to the kitchen and mops up the spillage with a tea towel, but it's too late; Noa's art is ruined.

I feel sick. "I'm so sorry." The tea has saturated the pile of art Mum chose. Noa's portrait of his dad is sopping wet and stained brown. I am the worst friend in the universe.

Noa scrambles to check his work. His fingernails scratch against the wooden table as he struggles to peel apart each stuck, sodden sheet. The sparkle in his eyes clouds over; every single piece is damaged.

A lump forms in my throat. "It's all my fault. I've wrecked your chance of getting into art school."

Noa avoids my eyes. "It was an accident."

Dad stands up. His jeans are splattered with tea. "*That* was the vision? Christ, why can't my bloody nephew save himself?" He splutters, "Why are these arsehole spirits besieging you?"

I sigh. "I don't know, Dad."

"Calm down, Simon. You're not helping." Mum

dabs the table with the tea towel. She turns to me. "Was this the real reason your window cracked?"

I nod. The pink neon sign comes back to me. "Flava? Where's that?"

Dad scoffs, "Flava? It's a gay bar off K' Road. Why? And what happened to your window?"

"Ask Mum."

Why can't this vision dump the clues on me all at once instead of leaving a few crumbs each time? It's making me suffer on purpose and now Noa's had to suffer, too. I have no doubt Vince is in danger. But what does the vision want me to do now? Go to Flava?

Mum holds up a tea-stained portrait of Noa's little sister Teuila and sighs. "This was one of my favourites."

"I'll re-do the best ones. I'm a fast worker and it's school holidays." There's a hard edge to his voice, like he's trying to hide how much of a disaster this really is.

I catch Mum's eye. She looks worried. "Why didn't you tell us, Marvel?"

"No point. There's nothing you can do."

"But you told Noa," Mum says, crestfallen.

I don't know what to say.

Dad hollers over from the kitchen where he's making himself another cup of tea. "Julia, she's seventeen for God's sake. It's her choice."

Mum's looks at me and gives a gentle nod.

"Please, don't worry about me," I say.

Noa gathers up the remains of his art and zips

up the plastic carry case. "Thanks so much, Julia." He stands to leave and glances over to me. "See you Friday, Marvel." He gives a stiff smile.

I stare out of the lounge window and watch Noa propel himself along the driveway. His art portfolio hangs off one crutch handle. I remember the beautiful portrait of his dad and swallow. That's not the kind of picture you can rush. I can't bear to think about him not getting into art school.

Julia frowns. "Isn't it odd? I just realised."

"What?" I say.

"My art exhibition is round the corner from Flava. What a coincidence."

It's no coincidence. I screw my eyes up and try to work out what I'm supposed to do with this information. I'm five foot two inches tall and I don't have a fake ID, so there's no chance I'll be allowed into a bar. Even if I could get in, when would I go and what would I do? Vince must avoid Flava and steer clear of anyone wearing a skull ring. If this vision can almost suffocate its messenger, then I dread to think what lies ahead for Vince if I can't convince him to believe me.

CHAPTER SEVEN

I clamber onto the bus with my skateboard strapped to my backpack, a bulky cardboard box in both hands and my Hop card between my teeth. I manoeuvre into a front seat and sit side-on with my backpack against the window and my legs draped across plush purple fabric. After four nights in a row of broken sleep, I feel like a zombie from one of those George Romero movies Dad and I like to watch. The psychic world is drilling its message home, disrupting my dreams with images of the skull ring, causing me to wake wide-eyed and sweaty in the dead of night. I'm wondering if this increased disturbance is all to do with timing. That whatever's going to happen to Vince is fast approaching. Waiting until Thursday to meet him has seemed like the longest week of my life.

The bus is stuffy and its gentle jolting lulls me, but I'm too anxious to sleep. The constant anticipation of the vision returning has transformed me into an adrenaline-fuelled wreck. My legs twitch and my shoulder muscles burn with tension. How much longer my body can handle being in this state isn't something I'm keen to explore. I'm holding out to deliver the vision's message to Vince in the hope the spirit world will grant me a well-earned break.

◆

Vince brushes the salon floor, making weary sweeps across the concrete. He's a lone hunched figure in a sea of scattered strands of hair.

"Hey, Vince."

His brush clatters to the floor. "Marvel! You gave me a fright." He hugs me and I feel his bony ribs pressing against my chest.

I step back and a ripple of shock goes through me. His unshaven face is gaunt and his jeans bunch up at the front where the pin of his belt buckle pokes through the furthest hole. I'm sure he wasn't this skinny last time.

"Are you alright? You look kind of stressed," I say.

Vince stares at me with a blank expression. "Money problems. It'll sort itself out."

"I brought your mum's stuff." I place Shirley's box on the reception desk.

His hand thumps against his chest and tears fill his eyes. "Thank you so much. That's so kind of you."

I take a sharp breath. There's a skull ring on his index finger. "I, err, I need to talk to you about something else." I can't take my eyes off it. It's identical to the one from the vision.

Vince follows my gaze and brings the ring up closer to my face. "You like it?"

I hesitate and think of the right words. "It's interesting." There is no way I got the hands mixed up. Vince wasn't wearing this ring in the vision. It was someone else.

"Grant had it specially made for my twenty-fifth birthday back in June." Vince tenses and fear crosses his face. "He gets mad if I don't wear it." He whispers, "To tell you the truth, I hate it. It spends most of the day in my pocket."

I don't think anyone could hate that ring as much as I do.

Vince picks up the broom from the floor. "Come back to mine, it's not far. I'll just finish tidying up."

"Alright." I study the skull ring on Vince's hand as it wraps around the broom handle and resist the urge to yank it from his finger and throw it out the front door.

By the time we reach the entrance to Vince and Grant's Freeman's Bay apartment, Vince is already on his third cigarette and we've only been walking fifteen minutes. To my relief, the skull vision hasn't made an appearance. Maybe it's because I'm with Vince and the interfering spirits are breathing a massive sigh of relief?

But the playground vision flashes up again just as Vince taps in the door code. A few seconds of kids playing. Such a pleasant respite from the skull ring vision, but it's odd that this one keeps recurring, too. I shake my head and follow Vince up the stairs. My hand runs along the smooth metal banister; it's the perfect set-up for a boardslide. Thoughts drift and I imagine sailing down the banister, flying off the end and nailing the landing. Nothing beats that feeling of pure exhilaration, of being free for a few blissful seconds. I glance up and sigh. Vince is waiting for me at the top of the stairs.

Vince's hallway's lined with charcoal-grey carpet and flanked by black walls. A blood-red console table stretches along the left side, its corners chipped, and one of the drawers is missing a knob. Unopened envelopes labelled *Final Demand* litter the table surface. Hanging from the ceiling is a black chandelier, but only half the bulbs work and it disperses uneven patches of light onto the walls. There's a bad smell like the rotten orange I once found hiding in the bottom of my backpack.

Vince shows me into the lounge. "Grant designed it. He calls it modern gothic. Drink?"

"Right. I'll have a Coke, please." I'm not sure if it's the depressing decor or the prospect of talking to Vince about the vision that's making me nervous. It's the same jitters I get when skating a no-skate zone in town. The lure of exploring new turf combines with the risk a cop could walk around the corner and refuse to believe my lame excuses.

I sit on a bottle-green velvet sofa surrounded by more black walls and take slow deep breaths. Above the fireplace is an ornate gold mirror and in the alcoves on either side hang stuffed pheasants, their tails dusting the black painted floorboards.

Vince puts Shirley's box in the corner behind a huge black candle. Blobs of wax congeal along the candle's length and collect in the flanges of the black metal holder. He reaches into a glass cabinet and pulls out a bottle of vodka and a can of Coke. The neck of the vodka bottle rattles against his glass as he pours himself a large measure. He sits opposite me in a high-backed armchair and seems to shrink within its banks of dark leather. It strikes me that Vince looks like someone about to burgle this place rather than live in it.

He takes a long sip of his drink, then passes me the can of Coke.

I shuffle to the edge of the couch and lean towards him. "Do you know anyone with a skull ring like yours?"

"No. Grant said it was a one-off." He lights a cigarette and walks over to the window, shoving it open with his elbow. A plume of smoke escapes into a cloudy Auckland sky.

"Do you go to a bar called Flava?"

He turns to me. "Ha. It's my second home. I'm there most weekends. Why?" His cigarette tip glows on his inhale and his cheeks suck in, making his face skeletal.

I screw my eyes up. *I hate this bit.* "A vision's been

appearing to me. I see Flava bar. You're in it and there's someone wearing that ring," I point to Vince's hand, "who intends to hurt you."

Vince shrugs. "I don't care." He knocks back the rest of his vodka, then walks over to the drinks cabinet and pours himself another. "I've had a life of hurt. Add it to the pile."

The can crumples in my hand. "I'm getting a heads-up. Don't you want to avoid it happening?"

"I can't change what's fated." He waves his glass in the air and vodka spills out.

I look into his bloodshot eyes and control the urge to yell. "You have free will. You have a choice."

Vince shakes his head and gulps down vodka.

A loud knock makes me jump.

"Grant must've forgotten his key." Vince's words slur. He swerves across the lounge.

I follow him and peer into the hallway. Another ear-splitting bout of knocking starts up.

"Alright, I'm coming." Vince opens the door.

The man flashes Vince his ID badge. "I'm here on behalf of the bank. Are you Grant Dickson?"

The man seems to be missing a neck; his jowls sag over the collar of his white shirt like the overweight Shar Pei who lives next door to Sadie.

"No. I'm his partner," says Vince.

"Long-term partner? More than three years?" he barks.

Vince nods.

The man thrusts an envelope into Vince's hand. "Repossession order. You've got fifteen days to vacate the property."

Vince closes the door. His glass of vodka slips from his hand, catches the edge of the console table and shatters, splashing ice-cold vodka over my legs.

I steer Vince around the broken glass. "You go and sit down. I'll clean it up." He's shaking and he clutches my arm so tight I wince.

I lead Vince back to the armchair. Inside the drinks cabinet I spy another can of Coke and reach inside to grab it. As I pull out the can, my hand knocks against something, sending it rolling into a glass tumbler. I peer between the glass shelves and a shiver goes through me. The community constable showed us one of these at school. It's a glass meth pipe. The bulbous end is coated with a layer of black soot. I hand Vince the Coke and remember Dad's comment about him smoking pipes. Vince's life sure is one hell of a car crash.

A key turns in the front door.

I dash into the hallway. "Careful. Vince broke a glass." I look up and my body stiffens. Goosebumps prickle down my arms. The aura surrounding the man at the door is like nothing I've ever encountered before. It's hazy with black blotches and if auras had a health rating, this one would be on life support.

He steps forward and kicks a large shard of broken glass under the console table. The metal studs decorating his black boots glint beneath the chandelier. He smiles, flashing gleaming white teeth. "And who are you, sweetheart?"

I step back from the dark energy around him. "I'm Marvel. Vince's cousin."

His steely grey eyes weigh me up. "Simon's kid?"

I nod, crinkling my nose at the smell of his woody aftershave.

"How shit-faced is he?" He walks past me and into the lounge.

"I'll get rid of the glass," I say to Grant's back.

He doesn't respond.

The kitchen cupboards are sparse, with little in the way of food or crockery, and there's a stack of empty pizza boxes by the bin. I rummage in the cupboard under the sink and find a dustpan and brush underneath a clump of plastic bags.

The atmosphere in the apartment reminds me of the tense silence hanging in the air after the school bullies exhausted their stock of insults and had nothing left to throw at me. Eager to leave, I work fast; sweeping up broken glass and melting ice cubes, then stopping to tease out glass fragments stuck to the carpet. A splinter of glass punctures my hand and I yelp. A bleb of blood appears. I angle my hand underneath the brightest segment of the chandelier and try to find purchase on the tiny sliver.

Vince's voice carries from the lounge. "The bank's calling in the magazine debt. They're kicking us out in two weeks."

I can't decipher Grant's mumbling.

"Sadie already gave us loads." There's a pause, then Vince falters. "Don't go back to Alex. You promised you'd never leave me." His voice collapses into sobs.

Blood's dripping onto the hall carpet. Barbs of pain shoot through my skin as I fumble beneath the dim light. It's no use. I take a deep breath and walk into the lounge, striding through a fug of cigarette smoke to the window. "Sorry. I need good light. I've got glass in my hand."

Vince's mouth gapes open. *Did he forget I was here?*

Grant shoots me a cold look and passes me a box of tissues. "Don't get blood on the furniture or I'll be sending your grandmother the cleaning bill."

"Thanks." My eyes latch onto Grant's hands, which are clustered with rings. A large black onyx beetle ring, a silver and garnet ring, a silver spider; but no skull ring with ruby eyes.

Grant mutters about hating the sight of blood and leaves the room. The tension in the air lifts.

I grapple with the glass splinter, my fingers in a pincer grip, sliding in the relentless stream of blood until I finally remove it. *Thank God.*

"All done." I look at Vince. His head lolls against the armchair and drool drips from his chin. On the side table next to him, the bottle of vodka is almost empty. "Earth to Vince." I raise my voice a little.

He turns in slo-mo and squints at me with bloodshot eyes. "Oh, you off?"

I hesitate and consider one last reminder about the vision, but there's no point. The opportunity for meaningful conversation has passed.

I sigh. "See you, Vince."

He grunts and gives a limp wave.

I fiddle with the lock on the front door.

Grant's reedy voice behind me. "Give my regards to your grandmother, sweetheart."

I swivel around and glare. *I'm no one's fucking sweetheart.* "My name is Marvel."

His leering smile makes my skin crawl. He reaches over me to unlock the door, smothering me with aftershave vapour tinged with sweat.

I stumble through the door and down the stairs, taking them two at a time, my body jolting with each downward step. My hand skims the smooth banister and I forget about the boardslide. Eyeing my exit, I thump the heel of my hand against the lock release and shoulder barge the door.

I skate downhill through dusky light. Cool spring air whips my cheeks and my wheels plough through fallen cherry blossom. Beyond the rows of weatherboard villas, the city's towers rise up like a protective shield. My rumbling wheels merge with the white noise of car engines and chatter of passersby. The miles of pavement between here and home should be long enough to soothe my troubled mind. I don't know whether warning Vince was enough to stave off the vision, but I'm not stopping to find out.

Obstacles block my path. A rolling drink can, followed by a twin pushchair and closer to home, a loose sheet of newspaper jams my wheels. Barriers all the way, disrupting my rhythm when what I really need is a smooth ride.

◆

I squeeze past a stack of Mum's art in the hallway. It's labelled and wrapped, ready for her exhibition tomorrow night.

In the lounge, Mum places a large canvas on the dining table and Sadie cuts a length of bubble wrap from a huge roll.

Sadie looks me up and down. "Marvella, you look exhausted. I'll put the kettle on. Put your feet up."

Mum finishes packaging up the painting. "How did it go with Vince?" She pushes a few loose strands of hair from her face.

"Not great." I sigh. "And even worse after he drank half a bottle of Smirnoff."

Mum's face falls. "Oh."

Sadie passes me a mug of tea.

I glance at Sadie. "I talked to Vince. He thinks whatever's going to happen can't be changed." All the turmoil I've been through over the last few weeks seems pointless.

Sadie sits on the couch opposite me. "The problem is Vince's state of mind. Nothing you say to him will alter that." Her gaze lifts to the lounge window. "I've tried many times to persuade him to seek professional help."

A horrible thought shoots cold dread through me. "Will Vince's state of mind derail Shirley's prediction?"

A flash of annoyance crosses Sadie's face. "For goodness sake, have faith in yourself, Marvella."

I stare at the floor. *I wish I could.* Another thought strikes me and I meet Sadie's eyes. "And to make matters worse, the bank's taking his flat."

Vince's world seems to be spiralling downwards, like when I lost control of my skateboard going down the Bullock Track. My exhilaration turned to sheer terror as I careered down one of Auckland's steepest streets. I stuck my back foot out to brake but got bad speed wobbles, and wide turns were a no go as cars headed up the opposite side. My board took on a life of its own and my fate twisted into a survival mission. Battling to resume some agency, I avoided smashing onto concrete by bailing into a thicket of prickly shrubs. And it's not the pain I remember, but my relief at being alive.

"It's actually Grant's flat. *Edge* must've finally gone under." Sadie sighs. "That's not good news for the equity investor. What's his name again?"

"Alex. His name's Alex." I take a sip of tea, remembering Grant's threat to leave Vince for him. "What's an equity investor?"

Mum says, "It's someone who invests money in

exchange for a share of the company." She sends Sadie a sympathetic look. "You won't get your money back either."

"It's alright, Julia. I resigned myself to that a long time ago."

Irritation sparks. "And Grant had the cheek to suggest Vince ask you for more money."

Sadie looks confused. "No one's asked me for any money."

Dad marches in. "Mother, under no circumstances should you give any more money to those two half-wits."

I snap, "Vince isn't a half-wit. None of this is his fault." I think about Grant and shudder at the memory of his sneering smile.

I slurp my tea, breaking the silence in the room. "Losing the flat's the least of Vince's problems." My voice trembles and sympathy for Vince surges through me.

Dad wanders over to the kitchen and places his empty mug on the bench. He fishes out the teabag and dumps it in the sink. "I take it Vince didn't believe you?"

"Yep." And I have this awful feeling the vision's going to keep kicking my ass until he does.

The pink neon sign of Flava nightclub flashes up and I swallow. If Vince is in no fit state to make decisions, then I need to make them for him. I'm going to pay Flava a visit after all.

CHAPTER EIGHT

The art gallery is hot and charged with excitement. Laughter rings out and smells of perfume and white wine drift across me. I move to Noa's side and point to a space over in the far corner. "Let's head over there."

He nods. His mouth gapes open as he takes in the size of the crowd.

I forge a path through, passing clusters of well-dressed people shuffling from one painting to the next. After another night of broken sleep, my tired eyes smart from the bright light and heat.

My voice strains with the effort to be polite. "Excuse me. Thanks." A middle-aged couple grumble and move just far enough apart to let Noa and I pass.

I spot Dad in the opposite corner, his shoulder hunching against one earphone as he positions a record on the turntable. I can barely hear his music over the hubbub.

I grab a plastic chair for Noa and stash his crutches in the corner.

He stares at a canvas on the wall behind me. "That's an amazing piece. Twelve hundred bucks. Sheesh." He squints at the title printed onto a small cardboard square beneath it. "*Rifts and The Passage of Time*. Do you know what it's about?"

I turn around. It's the painting Mum was working on when I barged in on her that day. Waves of yellow and blue flow the full length of the canvas, splattered with dots of red. A green sticker, indicating it's been sold, is stuck on the wall. "I don't really understand her art," I say, front teeth grazing my lip. I know my experiences are an influence, but how she can create such stunning art is beyond me, because being psychic sucks.

Noa stares at the painting, completely absorbed in its ripples of colour. And I wonder if this is what Mum meant about taking the viewer on a journey.

In his black T-shirt and black jeans, Noa fits right in with the art crowd. Unlike me, in four-day-old jeans and a creased, faded T-shirt. I haven't even brushed my hair.

The wine table is by my elbow and I take a glass from one of the rows and hand another to Noa. I gulp it down. The cool, syrupy liquid disperses through my body, taking the edge off my nerves.

Mum comes over. Her eyes shine and her fair hair sweeps around her shoulders. She leans in to Noa and points to a man in a flowery shirt. "That man over there, he's one of the lecturers at Whitecliffe College. Might be worth introducing yourself?"

Noa blows out air and wipes his palms down his thighs. "Okay. I've never done this kind of thing before."

"Come on. I'll introduce you." Mum passes Noa his crutches.

"Go, Noa. I'll be fine." I reach over to the table and take another glass of white wine. My heart hammers in my chest and I feel sick with anxiety, knowing this is an opportunity to sneak out.

Noa hauls himself up. "Alright. See you in a bit, Marvel."

I watch him disappear into the crowd.

A chemical smell surrounds me and I sniff my wine, then slam back against the wall as realisation hits me. "Go away," I mumble. The neon Flava sign appears. Curvy pink letters fill my field of vision and my throat tightens. I slide down the wall and land on hard, slippery concrete. I press the cold glass against my forehead until the vision disappears, then chug back the rest of the wine.

I grasp a leg of the plastic chair and hoist myself into it. I glance up and a lady looks at me over the top of her glasses and shakes her head.

I stagger into the toilets. Muffled sound transmits through the walls and my ears ring. I fill my empty wine glass with water from the sink and down three glasses. My appearance in the harsh light of the mirror shocks me. My face is washed out and there are dark circles under my eyes, like how I looked when I got glandular fever in Year Ten. I splash my face with cold water and rub my cheeks to bring some colour back. Above the mirror is a brass clock. Its hands are stopped. Water drips down my face and the Flava sign reflects back at me. I screw up my eyes and grip the edges of the sink. The ammonia smell makes me retch and vomit splatters into the basin. By the time I stop heaving the vision's gone.

I yank a paper towel from the dispenser and wipe my mouth, then run the tap to wash away the vomit. Two visions in five minutes. I'm not waiting for a third.

I jostle through the crowd, jutting out my elbows in my desperation to escape before another vision strikes. A man spills his wine and tuts at me. Dad's electronic music bleeps and chimes in the background as I forge towards the exit. I lunge for the door and stumble into fresh night air.

I scan both sides of the street. *Where's Flava?* I look up into light-polluted sky and mutter, "You've scared the shit out of me. The least you can do is help me find it." I start spinning and reach to a wall for support.

I remember Mum saying it was around the corner from the gallery. I make a beeline for the nearest side street and try to walk in a straight line. Placing one foot in front of the other is an effort. The smell of fried food drifts out from a takeaway shop and it dawns on me that I haven't eaten any dinner. I need to soak this booze up with something, else I'm never going to make it to the bar.

In the window of a disused office space I shovel down chips. They taste so good. Hot and salty morsels of potato slide down my throat, warming my belly. People stream past me, their clattering heels and laughter drowning out the traffic noise. I crumple up the empty bag and stuff it inside a bin.

There's a sex shop on the corner of the side street, its door covered in stickers, backlit from the strip lights inside. Each sticker displays a topless woman advertising massage and a phone number. *So gross.* I take the side street, into the shadow of warehouses and metal shutters. A gust of wind blows a takeaway cup against my Vans and I kick it into the road. Further down the street, on the left-hand side, a pink sign glows. It's the beacon I'm searching for, the one that's been plaguing my dreams and disturbing my sleep all week: *Flava.*

There's a loud groan behind me and I glance back up the street. A drunk guy staggers along the opposite pavement, his back to me. He's so far gone his friend supports him by wrapping an arm around his waist. The drunk man doubles up, like he's about to spew. His knees buckle and his flailing arms turn cartwheels through the air. The other man curses and hustles him into a car parked along the main road. He shoves, then kicks the drunk man's legs into the footwell and yanks the seatbelt across him. Doors slam and the car accelerates from the kerb. The drunk guy in the passenger seat glances over and a chill passes through me. It's Vince.

I race up to the main road and crane my neck in the car's direction. In the distance, its brake lights glow as it speeds around a corner, out of sight. I squat with my head in my hands, gripped by an ominous feeling that twists my guts. I'm pretty sure my job was to prevent Vince getting in that car. Major fail.

A sharp tap on my shoulder. "Marvel! I've been looking for you everywhere."

I swivel around to face Noa. The sudden movement triggers off the spinning again and I place both palms on the pavement to steady myself.

"She's had a few," a male passer-by mutters, then bursts out laughing.

My face burns as I grasp Noa's outstretched hand and haul myself to standing. "I saw Vince. He was out of it. This guy put him in a car and drove off." I swallow down the lump in my throat and the nagging thought that whatever could have gone wrong just has.

Noa's eyes bore into me. "Did you go to that bar from your vision? The one you said Vince hangs out in?"

I exhale and look down. The pavement beneath me sways and waves of nausea start up. I focus on a shop front opposite and wait until the nausea passes.

Noa shakes his head. "Why didn't you tell me? Why do you insist on dealing with everything yourself?"

"I'm sorry. I blew it. I've messed up everything." Tears well over. "After you got hurt, I was determined to stop what was destined for Vince. He's too depressed to care, so I went to look for him, but I was too late."

Noa hesitates. "Wait here." He goes into the dairy a few doors up and returns with a bottle of water. "Here."

"Thanks." I twist off the cap and take a sip.

"Are you certain it was Vince?" A group of singing women steam past. One of them brandishes a bottle of champagne. "I mean, it's Friday night. Everyone's pissed." He avoids my gaze and I guess his observation includes me.

I lock eyes with Noa. "It *was* Vince." Guilt swamps me. It's like Noa's fall's happening all over again. *Why did I stop for chips?*

Inside the art gallery, only a few stragglers remain. A tired-looking server collects up the empty wine glasses and places them inside a plastic crate. Over in the DJ booth, Dad's ditched the mellow electronica and is back in his comfort zone, playing Indie rock.

He comes over. "Where did you disappear to?"

I place a hand lightly on Noa's arm. "I needed some fresh air."

Dad raises his eyes and glances at Noa. "Thanks for looking after her, mate." He cups a hand around his mouth. "Poncy lot, the art crowd. Though the wine seems to have loosened a few wallets."

Mum's arm snakes around my shoulders. "Pardon, Simon?" She fires him a sharp look.

I drag my thoughts away from Vince and force a cheery tone. "How did it go, Mum?"

Her eyes glisten. "Great. Sold three and lots of

interest. And Noa had a nice chat with the chap from the art school."

"Yeah, he was cool. Gave me a few tips for my application." Noa smiles. "Thanks, Julia."

At least some good came out of tonight.

I close the taxi door and tell Mum and Dad I'll be in soon.

Noa asks the driver to wait a minute, then hauls himself out of the front seat and stands opposite me.

The alcohol's worn off, leaving me with a throbbing pain in my head and a heart soaking in regret. I drain the rest of the water from the bottle Noa bought me.

It's gone midnight and the street is deserted. No lights are on inside Sadie's and I stare into the shadows beneath her verandah, knowing tomorrow I'll have to confess what happened.

"Have you got Vince's mobile?" says Noa.

I sigh. "I tried in the taxi. It goes straight to voicemail."

"What are you going to do?"

I look into his kind brown eyes and realise any doubt he had about what I saw has gone. Even without any proof something bad's happened to Vince.

"If I don't hear back, I'll talk to Sadie in the morning. See if she has Grant's number."

"Promise me *again* you'll keep in touch. If anything happens, text."

"I promise." I hug him, wrapping my arms tightly around his back and wish I didn't have to let go.'

CHAPTER NINE

I wake from the best sleep I've had in weeks and within seconds, dread hits me like slamming my board into a block wall. I bolt upright and grab my phone off the side table. Vince hasn't replied to any of my calls or messages.

I dress in last night's clothes and race out of the house to Sadie's. I trip and bash my shin on her steps in my haste to reach the front door. My fist hammers against wood. The sound echoes up the street and sets off next door's dog, who barks like he wants to tear me to shreds. Dire scenarios about Vince's welfare career though my mind.

Finally, I hear footsteps and the door clicks open.

"Have you got Grant's mobile?" I say, catching a breath.

Sadie looks at the floor and tugs at the silver chain around her neck. "The police already phoned." She steps aside to let me in. "Vince has been kidnapped. Grant received a ransom text this morning." Sadie paces back and forth across the lounge, her heels clicking rhythmically against the floor like a ticking clock.

My arms and legs stiffen and I slowly lower myself onto the couch. "I failed."

Sadie gets the full story, minus the alcohol and detour to the chip shop. The mere memory of those events makes me shiver with shame.

She stops pacing. "Think, Marvel. Take your mind back. Surely you got some details—car colour, registration?"

I bite my lip. "It was dark."

Sadie has a puzzled expression and I wonder if she's trying to fathom out why her faith in me backfired so dramatically.

She sits in the armchair and says firmly, "Don't worry. This isn't over yet."

I frown. "What do you mean?"

Sadie doesn't answer. She stares through the lounge window and there's a steeliness in her blue eyes that I've never seen before.

She passes me a Post-it note. "You need to contact this chap. He's the detective on the case. John Edmonds. Tell him what you saw."

I take a sharp breath in. "He won't believe me."

Sadie's expression doesn't change. "Probably not about the visions, no."

I swallow down my fear and take the note. Sadie's shaky copperplate loops across the lime-green paper. *Detective Inspector John Edmonds, Auckland CIB.*

I point to the phone number beneath the writing. "Is that a one or a seven?"

Sadie squints. "A seven."

I pull out my phone and try to stop my hands shaking. "Okay. Here goes."

◆

Drops of rain splash my arms as I skate the final corner to Noa's house. The sky darkens and rain falls in slanting rods. I run up Noa's driveway with my skateboard sliding under my arm and the earthy smell of wet ground all around me. Sheltering beneath the roof overhang, I ring the doorbell. Watery dirt from the skateboard wheels drips down my arms and strands of damp hair stick to my face. A roll of thunder startles me. The playground vision comes back. Two boys in raincoats on swings, their laughter breaking through dull grey sky—a sky like today's.

"Ground control to Marvel." Noa leans on the doorframe with his arms folded like he's been waiting a while. His mouth forms a wide smile.

My heart does a flip. It's the same rush of emotion as last night's hug. I force it from my mind. Life is complicated enough as it is. "Sorry. That one was only a few seconds, wasn't it?"

"Yeah, about ten. I may as well not be here, because you stare right through me." He ushers me inside. "Not the skull ring one though, was it?"

I turn back to him. "No. That one won't be coming back and that's kind of why I'm here."

Teuila runs up to me and throws her arms around my waist. "Marvel's here!"

Doors open and feet patter down the hallway. The children surround me, becoming a barrier of shape-shifting bodies as they jostle each other for closest position.

"You must be Noa's girlfriend by now," says Isaia, splaying out his hands.

Tavita tugs on my damp T-shirt and points to a blood-soaked Band-Aid stuck to his right knee. "I hurt my knee. Look."

"Ugh, that's gross." Luisa screws up her face. "*Are* you Noa's girlfriend?"

Noa shoots her a look and she sinks her head.

Teuila grips my hand tight and leans her head against my arm.

I look down to her. "Teuila, I hear you got an award today?" As soon as the words leave my mouth, regret submerges me.

Teuila's smile broadens and she puffs out her chest. "Yes, for gymnastics."

"Err, well done," says Noa with a quizzical expression.

Isaia's mouth hangs open. "How did you know, Marvel?" He turns to Noa. "She can do magic. You *have* to be her boyfriend."

Noa winks at me. "She's a good guesser. They give awards out for fun these days."

Teuila looks disappointed.

I squeeze Teuila's small hand. "Well, I think you did great."

Isaia takes a step nearer. "You can't guess *that*. You're psychic aren't you? Like the boy in the movie, *The Sixth Sense*."

Noa clears his throat. "That's enough, Isaia." He hesitates, then crouches in front of his brothers and sisters. "Sometimes, Marvel does see the future."

The children gaze up at me, awestruck.

"But, you all must promise not to mention this to Mum. Because Mum doesn't believe in psychics and if she finds out, she won't want Marvel and me to be friends."

The children's faces fall.

Teuila's hand slips from mine.

Noa stands. "Marvel's here to help me with my work. Luisa, you're in charge until Mum gets home from work."

Tavita stamps his foot. "Aw, Noa, all you've done this week is work and work. You never play with us anymore."

Noa pats his arm and gives his youngest brother a sympathetic smile. "Portfolios don't draw themselves. Once I've finished, I'll help you build that fortress for your soldiers. I promise."

Tavita smiles and scarpers off down the hall.

Guilt renders me speechless and I stare at the shiny wooden floor. If Noa had any sense he'd ditch me while he can. Find a calm, non-weird friend who doesn't see into the future. Someone his Mum will actually like.

Noa's studio is a world away from the tidy space it was last time. There's a rank smell of body odour mixed with turps. Open tubes of acrylic paint and paint-hardened brushes are strewn across the table below the easel. Next to them are jars of dirty water and a half-drunk cup of coffee. Scrunched up paper, pie wrappers and empty chip packets litter the floor. *I hope he hasn't been working through the night?* He's sketched an outline of his father's face on the paper pinned to the easel and another wave of guilt crashes over me.

I balance on the table edge and Noa sits on the chair. We're so close our feet touch.

"What's happened?" he asks.

"Vince got kidnapped. The police want to talk to us about last night. The detective's coming to my house at four."

Noa straightens up. "Police want to talk to *us*? But I didn't see anything." He gazes out of the cracked, taped-up window, then turns back to me. "I can't. I need to finish my portfolio." His voice is clipped.

"Sorry, I told the detective you were with me—"

Anger flickers across his eyes. "Marvel, I found you *after* you saw Vince. What use am I?"

A lump forms in my throat and I move away from

the table. "I'll let you get on. I've caused you enough bother already."

Noa sighs. "It's not you." His tone softens. "The Salesas don't have a great track record with the cops."

Something in me snaps, like when I let rip at a boy who hijacked my turn on the skate ramp. Selfishness riles me and it's selfish of Noa to refuse to co-operate. "The police are the only people who can save my cousin. Every little bit of information helps."

I let the shed door slam behind me and wade through long grass, taking the long way around the house to avoid windows and prying eyes. No way can I face those kids and their silly questions about Noa being my boyfriend. Like that's ever going to happen.

It's hard to skate with tears in your eyes. They combine with thoughts to thwart me and I swerve off the kerb, jolting onto the road. A flash of speeding red metal and a rush of air; the car misses me by a fraction. I stumble back onto pavement and sit under a tree, waiting for my heart to slow and my mind to settle. One thought circulates in my head. It filters to the surface and takes priority over Noa and his reluctance to co-operate: I need to help find Vince. I shiver, thinking of him tied to a chair somewhere, cold and scared. A part of me is still holding on to Shirley's prediction. And since I failed to prevent Vince's kidnap, the least I can do is assist the police and tell them what I know.

CHAPTER TEN

Dad's singing along to The Clash's version of *Police and Thieves*. He's doing a mortifying Dad dance which involves shuffling his feet and some random shoulder tilting. His movements remind me of the Pinocchio string puppet Sadie bought me for my fifth birthday.

My head aches and weariness comes over me, but there's no way I can doze through the racket of jarring electric guitar and Dad's tuneless whining.

Sadie clears empty glasses and mugs from the dining table and plumps up the couch cushions. She sends me a sympathetic smile. "I filled in Simon and Julia about you seeing Vince last night."

"That's okay." I tug at a strand of cotton dangling from the edge of my denim cut-offs and snap it off.

"Turn it down, please. I'm a little delicate," says Mum from the kitchen. She knocks back two Panadol tablets and a glass of water, then picks up a pot of coffee and skulks off to her studio.

The song changes to *I Fought The Law* and I realise

Dad's got a police theme going on. And he's wearing a Clash T-shirt. *Oh, for God's sake.* "Dad, this music isn't helping to focus my mind. It isn't therapy. It's annoying."

"Have any spirits disturbed you today, Marvel?" He doesn't wait for me to answer. "No? Well, job done."

I bristle. "Your music can't take credit for that. It's never blocked any—"

A knock at the front door.

Sadie frowns at Dad and he turns off the music. She dusts fluff from her trousers and goes to answer the door.

I take the seat furthest from Dad at the dining table and take a deep breath. *I'm doing this for Vince.*

"Come through, Detective." Sadie extends her arm towards Dad, then me. "This is my son, Simon, and my granddaughter, Marvel." Sadie's using her posh phone voice.

"DI John Edmonds, Auckland Criminal Investigation Branch. Thanks for meeting me." He smiles and the skin around his eyes and across his forehead corrugates into thick folds.

Detective Edmonds sits at the head of the table. He loosens his tie, then sets down a notebook, some sheets of lined paper and a blue biro. It's a while before he speaks. Eventually, he casts his gaze around the table. "The ransom's three million New Zealand dollars, to be paid in bitcoin. Deadline seven p.m. next Friday."

I lean closer to hear his gravelly voice.

Dad sits up straighter. "Bitcoin? Christ, that's a bit advanced, isn't it?"

"Harder to trace. Runs on computer networks. Gets encrypted, so avoids traditional banking systems," Edmonds says in a monotone.

"Yeah, I know all about it." Dad frowns. "Isn't asking for bitcoin a little unusual?"

"It is, but so are kidnappings." He turns to me. "Marvel, I'm going to need a statement. As you are seventeen, a support person isn't mandatory but you're welcome to have your father and grandmother here if you wish."

I look from Dad to Sadie. "I'm fine on my own."

Sadie shoots Dad a sharp look. "You'll only get on your high horse about the visions, Simon. I think it best if I stay with Marvel."

Dad grunts. "I suppose there's some truth in that." He looks at Edmonds. "I'll leave you to it, Detective." He ambles across the lounge and opens the door to his office.

Edmonds checks his watch and writes at the top of one of the lined sheets of paper. He looks up. "Is that all okay with you, Marvel?"

"Yes. I suppose." I glance across to Sadie and force a smile, then turn back to Edmonds. "But you have to promise me something."

Edmonds tilts his head. "Go ahead."

I squeeze my hands together. "You'll keep an open mind."

After I've finished my statement, Detective Edmonds falls silent and chews the end of his pen. "These visions. I don't understand. Are they dreams?" His tone of voice is more curious than derogatory.

I sigh. "No—"

Sadie tuts. "They're most certainly not dreams. Marvella has experienced psychic visions since she was a small child."

Irritation rises up and I try to catch Sadie's eye, but she avoids me.

"Fascinating," says Detective Edmonds. He pauses. "Marvel, can you clarify how much wine you drank last night? It may affect the validity of your statement."

My face goes hot and I look down. "Two." I hesitate. "Err, they were quite large measures."

"That's a shame." Detective Edmonds taps his pen on the table. "What was the name of the person with you?"

"Noa. He came to look for me, but he only found me after I saw Vince."

"Full name?"

"Noa Salesa."

"Salesa?" His gaze drifts to the window and his brow furrows. He takes a card from the front pocket of his notebook and skims it across the table. "I'd appreciate a quick word with him."

"Okay." I swallow and stick the card in the back pocket of my jeans.

I study Edmonds' face, which until I mentioned

Noa's surname was inscrutable, but now displays a scowl. *Why is he angry with Noa?*

Edmonds writes something in his notebook.

Dad returns, nonchalantly humming a Clash tune, and slides into a chair. "Marvel's statement useful, Detective?" His voice lifts.

I roll my eyes at Dad.

"A little." Detective Edmonds forces a smile, then changes the subject. "I understand you're estranged from Vince Allen."

Dad shunts forward and his eyes narrow. "I was at the art exhibition with my wife. Ask anyone who was there."

Edmonds holds up his palms. "You're not a suspect. It was just a question."

Dad leans back. "My nephew is an alcoholic and a meth head. I dropped him years ago. He was pissed last night, wasn't he, Marvel?"

Edmonds interrupts. "Actually, Vince wasn't drunk last night." He looks from Dad to me.

My mouth gapes open. "But, he couldn't even—"

Edmonds raises a finger. "He had two vodkas in Flava. Witnesses in the bar say he wasn't inebriated. We suspect his drink was spiked and this is what incapacitated him."

"Anyone in there mention seeing a bloke with a skull ring, like the one bugging Marvel in her vision?" says Dad.

"We can't use that line of questioning. Psychic

phenomena are inadmissible and could compromise the investigation." Edmonds glances at me and smiles weakly, like he's apologising for official policy. And I wonder how closely he follows it.

Dad folds his arms across his chest. "Disbelieve my daughter at your peril. She's never wrong. Poor kid's been hounded by spirits all her life and no one bloody listens to her."

I rest a hand against my forehead. "Dad!"

"I didn't say anything about not believing Marvel. But I can't let anecdotal evidence override hard, cold fact." Edmonds inhales and turns to Sadie. "I understand you're close to Vince, despite not recouping your investment in *Edge* magazine. I've been informed the magazine is currently in receivership and—"

"We're not as close as we used to be, but that's nothing to do with losing the money. I knew it was risky." Her eyes brim with tears. "Vince has a lot of personal problems. It's all rather complicated. The magazine failing isn't Vince's fault. It all got too much and he left last year. Went back to hairdressing."

Detective Edmonds smiles at Sadie and gently steers the interview. "Why exactly did Vince leave *Edge*?"

"Grant." Sadie hesitates. "It's such a shame Vince couldn't bring himself to leave the relationship too." She looks away.

I shudder as I recall Grant's black diseased aura

and it's as if my brain is compensating for it, because the image from the first time I saw Noa flashes up: the unusually bright vision and his glowing white aura, so beautiful and strong. It was special. It was a one-off. I try to get a handle on my emotions because I can't cry here, not in front of Edmonds.

"Vince's styling made *Edge* a success but Grant was too controlling. Working with him drove Vince around the twist. That's why the other chap went to Australia." Sadie glances to me. "Marvel – what's his name again? I keep forgetting."

I sit forward in my chair. "Alex."

Sadie closes her eyes and shakes her head, like she's trying to loosen a memory.

Edmonds flicks through his notebook. "We know about Alex Weston. Owns fifty percent of *Edge*. He stands to lose a lot of money. Hasn't left Australia for five years. Dabbles in property development now."

Sadie's face brightens. "Oh yes, I remember now. He was one of Grant's ex-boyfriends—poor guy invested his entire inheritance. My loss is peanuts."

Detective Edmonds shuffles his papers together and prepares to leave. A question burns me but Dad beats me to it.

"Surely Grant's a suspect?"

Edmonds levels with Dad. "His alibi checks out."

"But he has a motive," I say.

"I never said Grant wasn't a suspect, but nothing ties him to the kidnapping. Vince has a history of drug use and mixes with some rough sorts—we're looking into his past."

Sadie lays both palms on the table and leans in. "The problem is, Detective, Vince has no money."

Detective Edmonds clears his throat. "Yes." He pauses. "And it's the policy of New Zealand Police not to pay ransoms." He stands, and I follow his gaze through the window to Sadie's beautiful white villa.

"If you need to get hold of me …" Edmonds lays a card on the table. "I'll keep you updated. Sadie, you'll be the main contact."

Sadie nods. Her face is tight with worry and no doubt the news I overdid the wine last night and stuffed my face with chips while Vince got kidnapped hasn't helped.

Dad shows Detective Edmonds out.

I move my chair closer to Sadie's and take her hand. It shakes in mine.

"I'm sorry I blew it." I hesitate and try to sound convincing. "They'll find him."

Sadie meets my gaze and shakes her head. "But they're not going to save him. That is up to you."

My jaw drops. How on earth am I going to do that? Not surprisingly, the psychic world's gone cold on me and I've nothing more to go on. No wonder Sadie's panicking. Judging by last night's disaster, there isn't a hope in hell of me saving anyone. Do I really trust the cops will find him? If Edmonds deems all the information from my visions irrelevant, then the outlook for Vince is even grimmer than I thought.

Dad strides across the lounge and clicks on the kettle. His smug grin drops when he sees Sadie's stricken face. "Mother, dear. Do not worry. I've got an idea."

"And what's that?" asks Sadie, standing up.

Dad taps a finger against the side of his nose.

Mixed emotions churn inside me. The last time Dad tried to help, he bollocked the bullies at my old school and it made the bullying ten times worse.

Sadie rests her hand on the back of the couch. "It's good you want to help Vince, but think of Shirley before you do anything rash. I don't want to lose a grandson as well as a daughter." She hooks her handbag over her forearm and walks with a slow, stooping gait towards the front door.

◆

I sit on my bed and write a text to Noa. *Hi, Sorry I stormed off. DI Edmonds asked if you'd call.* I type in the phone number and leave it at that. No emojis, no piss-takes, just a civil, bare bones text. However much I tell myself finding Vince is all that matters, thoughts of Noa push through, and despite our argument, he's still a beam of sunlight breaking through Auckland clouds.

A vision of a woman flashes up. She's writing at a desk under lamplight. Her soft features and dark hair are suffused in golden light. A baby sleeps in a cot by her side, its tiny pink hands curled up over a blanket. Above the desk is a picture I recognise, a print of Rembrandt's: *The Night Watch*. It hangs over the desk in Sadie's spare bedroom. I gasp. Is the woman Shirley, with baby Vince in the cot? Why is she appearing to me? *Has she come for Vince?*

I grab a school exercise book and sketch the image while it's fresh in my mind. I'm sure Sadie has a photo of Shirley by her bed. I'll go over first thing tomorrow.

CHAPTER ELEVEN

I find Sadie at the far end of the garden, pruning an overgrown shrub. She grimaces as her hands strain to close the secateurs around a thick woody stem. The bin at her side overflows with limp straggly weeds, its wheels sinking into the lawn. There's a smell of freshly cut grass which makes my nose tickle.

Sadie barks an order to Martin, her gardener and general handyman, who turns off the weed eater. "Sorry, Marvella. I can't hear a thing with that going. Could you climb in the bin and trample it down? I'd rather not ask Martin."

I didn't come over to be co-opted into gardening, but no way am I letting Martin, who's pushing eighty, do it. I stamp down the spongy foliage and the bin contents sink to halfway. From this vantage point I spot Agnes, Sadie's friend. She's cleaning the windows inside. On a Sunday. *What's going on?*

I jump down. My legs itch from the prickly greenery. "This is a bit full on for spring cleaning, isn't it?"

Sadie throws a bunch of stems into the bin. "They're coming to take photos tomorrow."

Cogs clunk into place in my mind. *Surely not?* "You're selling?"

"Short notice auction. Four o'clock next Friday. The bank have agreed bridging finance. It should sell for enough to pay Vince's ransom." There's a determined expression on her face, like when she told me I was going to save Vince. And so far, that's not working out too well. No wonder she wants a back-up plan.

"You don't trust the police to find Vince either, do you?"

Sadie scoffs, "Course not. That detective has barely anything to go on."

I stare at the freshly mown lawn and remember all the times I played here as a kid. Backyard cricket with Dad, swing ball and frisbee. All those happy memories will be tainted and it's all my fault. I wish the ground would swallow me up.

My voice shakes. "Where will you live?"

Sadie compresses the secateurs and grits her teeth. "I already spoke to Simon and Julia. I'll move into the spare room."

I glance at the white weatherboards, beautiful ornate fretwork and tall sash windows. "It's such a shame."

"You can't get sentimental about buildings. There is no better option." Sadie dumps more cuttings into the bin. "Did you come over for a reason, Marvella?"

"Yes. I need to look at something."

Martin starts up the weed eater and grass cuttings shoot into the air.

I point to the sky and imitate a movie, like I'm playing charades.

Sadie ushers me to the front of the house, where it's quieter. "What did you see?" Her eyes brighten with expectation.

"I saw a woman writing at the desk in your spare room and a baby in a cot. I think it was Shirley and Vince."

"Probably. They'd often stay with me. Shirley always wrote her journal late at night. It was the only peace she got. Your Uncle William hit the booze not long after breakfast. When cancer took Shirley, Vince lived with me, off and on." Sadie's eyes glaze with sadness. "I'm surprised William lasted as long as he did—his liver finally packed in."

I screw up my eyes. "So, why am I seeing her? It could mean Vince is already dead."

"Oh, goodness me. Why would her spirit appear to you if she's already with him? Don't you see?"

I open my eyes.

"Shirley doesn't want you to give up on saving her son. She came to give you hope."

"Then cancel the auction."

Sadie levels with me and smiles. "And as you know too well, Marvella, what spirits reveal isn't foolproof."

I clench my hands. "So, why did you tell me to have faith in myself?"

"Because I saw—"

A sleek black car pulls up in front of the house. Its black metal glints in the morning sun.

A chill passes through me. "Were you expecting someone?"

Sadie sighs. "It'll be the real estate agent."

A man in black jeans and T-shirt gets out. He's surrounded by shadow. "Shit. It's Grant." I whisper so sharply Sadie jumps.

Sadie pulls off her gardening gloves and walks up to meet him. Her voice is cool. "What do you want?"

Grant bows his head and offers her a ring-stacked hand. "You're looking well, Sadie. Despite such harrowing circumstances."

Sadie ignores his hand.

Grant's eyes lift to me and he nods. If he calls me sweetheart I'll lose it.

I stay near enough to hear but far enough to avoid the full impact of his aura. Even at this distance I'm freezing, and goosebumps pop along my forearms, tugging at my skin like tiny biting insects.

"Can we talk privately?" Grant asks Sadie, then glances at me.

"Here's fine." Sadie's voice is clipped. Bet she doesn't want to be trapped in a room with him either.

Grant forces a smile. "I came to discuss Vince's ransom. I'm sure you're keen to help your grandson."

Sadie doesn't answer. Tension hangs thick in the silence between them, broken only by the low drone of Martin's weed eater.

"You've had enough of my money." Sadie's voice is laced with bitterness.

Grant steps back. "I'm sorry your investment didn't bear fruit, but you knew the risk. You can't conflate that with the ransom money. It could cost Vince his life. And how would you feel then?"

I kick my toe against the post of Sadie's picket fence, going faster and harder as the urge to shout grows.

"I love my grandson. This whole debacle is best left to the police."

Grant rolls his eyes. "Auckland CIB are working their slow, painstaking way through the long list of low-lifes I gave them. You have no idea the people your dear grandson was mixing with." There's a smug tone to his voice, like this is a competition and he just got the upper hand. "He'll be withdrawing from meth and alcohol. I dread to imagine what state he's in. The poor boy." He dips his head.

Sadie stiffens and her shoulders hunch almost to her ears. "Goodbye, Grant."

Grant looks over. "See you, sweetheart."

I bound forwards, fists clenched and barrel straight into Sadie's outstretched arm.

She looks at me and shakes her head.

A spray of water tickles the back of my legs. "Oh, sorry, love. I haven't got my glasses on." Agnes rubs a cloth against Sadie's lounge window.

Martin shouts over. "All done, Sadie. Ready for the photos."

Damn.

Grant sneers and I feel sick to the stomach. He runs a hand through his slick grey hair, then walks back to his car, biker boots clacking against the driveway.

With a shaky hand, Sadie tucks strands of white hair behind her ears. "Isn't he awful?"

"His aura freaks me out. It's all black and blotchy."

Her voice trembles. "What has Vince got himself into?"

I hug Sadie. Her arms are too stiff to hold me, they press lightly against my hips. I listen to her trembling breaths and stare across the street. The faint smell of Grant's woody aftershave hangs in the air. One thought dominates. It's the strongest feeling of knowing I've ever had. *Grant's involved and I'm going to prove it.*

I pull away from Sadie and force a smile. "Cup of tea?"

Sadie exhales. "Lovely. One for Martin and Agnes, too, please."

I walk down the hallway, holding the tea tray tightly in both hands. Sadie's best china clinks and rattles. Tea spills onto the tray from the overfilled teapot. The faint buzz of the weed eater carries from the front yard. I stop by Sadie's spare room and glance in. Dust motes are suspended in a shaft of sunlight which lights up the desk where I saw Shirley writing.

In Sadie's bedroom, I leave the tray on her bed and pick up the framed photograph on her bedside table.

Shirley's cradling Vince in her arms. She looks serene and her eyes radiate love. There's no doubt she's the woman from my vision.

I carry the tray outside, towards the roar of the water blaster.

Martin's aiming the nozzle a few metres from the front door. A ray of sun creates rainbow colours through the spray. I fixate on the pretty colours and the vision flashes up of the two boys on swings. Their laughter rings out, dulling the noise of the water blaster. Beyond them is a row of white-rendered townhouses. This one keeps coming back, yet the skull ring vision has stopped. I lurch forward and almost drop the tray. *How could I be so stupid?*

My phone buzzes in the pocket of my denim cut-offs. I place the tray on the top step. *Please be Noa.*

It's Detective Edmonds. He gets straight to the point and explains in his low gravelly voice that a witness from Flava remembers seeing a man in sunglasses wearing a skull ring. CCTV from the street wasn't helpful.

I fist punch the air. "Good you checked."

"Could be coincidence. The witness didn't see the man talking to Vince." He gives me the official line again about psychic stuff not standing up in court, then he pauses and his voice goes quiet, making it hard to hear. I jam a finger in my other ear.

"Let me know if you see anything relevant. We need all the help we can get. Day or night."

A shiver goes through me. To ask for my help means he must be getting desperate. "Okay." The playground vision comes to mind but it's too vague. The last thing I want to do is send the police down blind alleys searching for this place.

His voice becomes stern. "Is your Dad back from his radio show?"

I crane my neck along the driveway and spot his parked car. "Yes, why?"

"Ask your father." He says a curt thanks and hangs up.

Dad's dozing in the armchair. A maudlin tune plays in the background. There's an empty beer bottle on the side table and it's not even lunchtime.

I shake his arm. "What did Edmonds want?"

Dad twitches and opens one eye. "Aren't you supposed to take a shower with your clothes off, not on?"

"Dad!" I exhale. "I accidentally walked into the path of a water blaster, alright."

He straightens up. "Okay, okay. Chill." He burps and the space between us fills with the stench of stale beer. "Esteemed Detective Edmonds gave me a bollocking." He splays out his hands. "I was only trying to help."

I close my eyes momentarily. "What happened?" I brace myself.

He looks sheepish. "I did an appeal for Vince on my radio show."

My gaze lifts to the ceiling and I shake my head.

Dad rolls his eyes. "Edmonds is pissed off I didn't run it past him. He's worried too much media interest may panic the kidnapper."

"Dad, you're a flipping journalist. How could you be so dumb?"

He folds his arms behind his head. "Yes. Edmonds summed it up nicely. He told me I was 'a fucking journalist gone rogue'. I quite liked that."

"This isn't a game, Dad."

He leans towards me, his face serious. "Marvel, I don't agree with their tactics. The more media fuss the better."

Dad wading in is like when this kid, Jim, rides his BMX through the skate park. All you can do is watch the chaos unfold as he ploughs across ramps, forcing skaters to scram and sending little kids fleeing to their parents, while hoping his antics will be over with soon.

I level with him. "Is it also because you don't want Sadie to sell her house?"

Dad grimaces. "Obviously, I don't want Vince to die. I'm not completely heartless. But living with my mother would drive me up the wall."

"For God's sake, Dad." I flounce off. If this does represent a softening of his grudge against Vince, then it's one hell of a double-edged sword.

"Oh, fuck," says Dad.

I push against my bedroom door and glance back.

Dad's fiddling with his phone. "And we're off. Forty missed calls and a shitload of texts. The media circus has begun." He meets my gaze and smiles like he just won Lotto.

I press my back against my bedroom door until it clicks shut. So much has happened. And now Dad's meddling with the investigation. I feel overwhelmed with a longing to talk to Noa, the only person apart from Sadie who really understands. A horrible sadness drifts over me at the memory of my outburst. It's been radio silence since. The thought of losing his friendship is unbearable. I grab my phone and text.

Can we meet? I owe you an apology. This time I follow my words with a line of sorry emojis.

He texts straight back: *Sure. Tomorrow good.* And follows it with a smiley face.

Relief sweeps through me and I flop back onto the bed.

CHAPTER TWELVE

I open the front door and freeze. "What's going on?" I whisper. A group of people clutching microphones and cameras stand at the far end of the driveway, blocking my way out.

I duck into Sadie's backyard and scramble over her freshly pruned box hedge. I tap on her window.

She opens the back door and rolls her eyes. "I daren't leave the house. They're like a swarm of bees."

"Aren't they trespassing? Did you phone the cops?"

"Yes, yes. Still waiting." She ushers me inside. "I've so much gardening yet to do. Oh, you wouldn't believe their questions. Raking up our family's past."

She pulls at her necklace, then walks over to the window and parts the net curtains with a shaky hand. "Oh, thank God, the police are here."

"Edmonds?"

"No, they look young. Constables, probably."

I go to the window and watch the group shuffle

past, camera gear slung over their shoulders. In their wake, two takeaway coffee cups roll across the pavement and onto the road. Two police officers get into a patrol car and drive away.

Sadie turns to me. "Edmonds rang before." She hesitates. "It's on tomorrow's front page and tonight's news."

My thoughts are interrupted by hammer knocks reverberating from Sadie's front yard.

I follow her to the door.

Outside, cameras click and a reporter thrusts a microphone into the face of a man in a baseball cap who's busy installing a *For Sale* sign on Sadie's lawn.

"How do I know if it's going to bloody sell? I'm not the agent. Bugger off," the man yells. He knocks the microphone out of the reporter's hand, slams the door of his ute and roars off down the street.

Sadie closes the door and sighs. "Well, there's a nice new angle for them."

If these journos are anything like Dad, once they get a bit between their teeth they won't let up. I'm sure plenty of people from my old school will talk about me in exchange for publicity. If the press discover I'm psychic, this story will roll on and on. Worst of all, it distracts the police from finding Vince, and time, however much I hate it, ticks on.

I open the front door. "Looks like the coast is clear." I glance back. "See you later."

◆

Morning sun filters through new leaves, dappling the path through the park. A pair of geese waddle away from my rumbling wheels and honk at me. I shift my weight and adjust my feet just in time for the approaching bend. It's an effort to focus, because the closer I get to my special place the more my heart pounds.

I shove my board under my arm and wade through long, wet grass. All around me is birdsong and the faint hum of Auckland traffic. I stop. Noa's already here.

Headphones squash his curls and he lifts a lime-green drink can to his lips, then rests it on the splintered wooden arm of my favourite bench.

I wipe my sweaty hands on my jeans and join him. "Hi."

"Hey, Marvel. Good to see you." He hugs me and his soft curls brush my cheek. Tinny music in my ears as his headphones slip off.

My breath streams out in a long exhale over his shoulder.

He pulls away and there's dark circles under his eyes. "I want to apologise for last time. I was out of line."

I swallow. "It's okay. I'm sorry I snapped." I pause. "I feel so bad about ruining your art."

"It's alright. I got the portfolio finished. And work

want me a few extra days in the hols which is good—should cover the art supplies."

Damn. Didn't even think about that. "I could've asked Mum. She's got loads of paints she never uses."

Noa smiles. "They're probably oils. Take way too long to dry." His gaze shifts to the trees in front and he cracks his knuckles, then turns to me. "There's something I need to tell you."

I hold his gaze and my fingernails dig into the wooden slats beneath me.

"I heard your Dad's appeal yesterday at work and thought if he can overcome his issues, then so can I. So, I phoned Edmonds." He bites his lip. "My cousin Luke's a suspect in the kidnapping." He inhales. "He sold Vince meth. Edmonds remembers him from when he worked in organised crime and drugs." He sinks his head.

"I'm sorry."

Noa nods. "I haven't seen him since Dad's funeral." He sighs. "Cops found tons of texts between Vince and Luke. None in the past few months, though."

"I found a pipe in Vince's apartment. Maybe he's got a new dealer?"

Noa shrugs. "No idea."

A thought springs. "Does Luke wear a skull ring?"

"Doubt it, his mum'd kill him." Noa shakes his head. "She's even more religious than mine. He'd never get away with a death symbol on his finger."

"She knows about him selling drugs?"

Sadness dulls his eyes. "Yeah. She told my mum she lights a candle in church for Luke every day."

I pat his hand. "Every family has its troubles."

He goes to put his arm around me.

I jerk forward. "Oh." The playground vision returns, like it's reminding me not to forget about locating it. *Bad timing.*

"Sorry. It came back."

Noa's eyebrows raise. "What did?"

I describe the scene to him. "I saw it when I was at your house on Saturday."

He frowns. "Sounds like Hobsonville Point." He swallows. "That's where Luke lives." Noa covers his face.

My voice shakes. "It's just coincidence."

He pulls his hands away. "It's a pretty strange coincidence. Everything you see is significant." His eyes bore into mine and it strikes me that Noa has more faith in my visions than I do.

"I can't be a part of this. I never told you Luke lives there, okay?" His voice is cool and his gaze shifts back to the trees. He stands and smiles weakly. "I'd better get going. I've got a fortress to build for my brother."

I glare. "You're jumping to conclusions. I'm going to bus out there and check. Auckland's teeming with new housing; land's being sliced up all over the place."

Noa takes a sharp breath in. "You can't go alone. No way. Luke has gang links, they have guns. You could end up getting kidnapped yourself, raped— God knows."

"Edmonds will have questioned Luke already. Has he been arrested and charged?"

"No, but …"

I stand in front of him. "I'm going to Hobsonville Point whether you come with me or not." I hesitate. "I promised Edmonds."

Noa's eyes widen. "Promised him what?"

"I'd report any relevant visions."

"If it is Hobsonville, then it doesn't look good for Luke, does it?"

"You're being paranoid." Anger bubbles up. "I don't get you. If Luke's involved, wouldn't you want him caught?" My voice is sharp.

Noa sits back down on the bench. "I don't want to argue." His eyes plead. "Let me come with you. I'm working at the cafe for the next few days, but I'm off Friday."

Friday night's the deadline. I hesitate. "Alright, but we leave early."

Noa exhales. "Okay." He reaches out for my hand and I pull him up. His grip is strong and warm.

I pull his crutches out of the grass and hand them over.

He looks at me and sighs. "There's a lot at stake for both our families." Worry flickers across his eyes.

For a moment, I consider abandoning my plan. Maybe, I should leave it all to the police? I've caused Noa enough bother. And now I'm forcing him to choose between me and his family.

I grab his arms. "Are you sure about coming with me?"

He kisses my forehead. "Yep."

The kiss gives me a sweet buzz and I lose my train of thought. Regaining my composure, I manage to keep my voice level. "Cool. See you Friday at eight."

CHAPTER THIRTEEN

I peer out the lounge window for any sign of reporters. Dad's ancient Honda Civic blocks the driveway, limiting my view, but there doesn't seem to be anyone lurking around. No doubt they'll be back in force later for Sadie's auction. I glance over to her house and sadness washes over me.

A car door slams and Noa stands at the end of the driveway, leaning on his crutches.

I grab my skateboard and backpack and close the door quietly behind me.

"Hey, Marvel. Have you seen the front page?" Noa tugs a newspaper from his back pocket and unrolls it.

I skim the print. "The press are loving it, aren't they? The auction, the kidnapping deadline, the ex-hairdresser of the year." Thank God there's no mention of me being psychic. I'll have to go into hiding if they find out about that. I hand Noa the paper. "Ready?"

Dark clouds gather in the distant sky and a gust

of wind sends curled up leaves and a chocolate bar wrapper into my path.

He nods and points a crutch in the direction of the bus stop. "Come on, it's going to piss down." Noa glances over. "Have you seen the playground vision again?"

A shiver goes down my spine. "Every day this week." It's recurring more often, just like the skull ring vision did.

The sky's darker now, ominous, like a bad spirit sent to sabotage the day. Drops of rain fall, light at first, then morphing into fat droplets which soak through my T-shirt.

I look behind me and squint at Noa. "Can you go any faster?"

"I'll try." He sticks his head down and propels himself through the deluge.

A roll of thunder makes me jump and a crack of lightning blitzes the sky. Black expanses of water ripple across the pavement, too wide to jump over. My soaking trainers squeak like a child's toy and my undone laces whip the pavement, splashing water up my legs. Sodden jeans stick to my thighs, weighing me down. The bus shelter is still at least a hundred metres away.

Noa pants hard alongside me and the rubber ends of his crutches splash into puddles. "Not far now," he says.

A sudden burst of energy comes over me. I pick

up speed and leave Noa behind. Panic surges through me, compelling me to run as if my life depends on it. A vision of a burning building appears. People are trapped inside, hammering at the windows and smashing through glass. The sound of screaming and yelling echoes around me, pushing me to go faster. The cacophony quietens and becomes a single human lament, like the whine of an injured animal in the dead of night. It's Vince's voice. His life's at stake.

I pull up short, like hitting a wall, a burning pain in my feet as they shear against the soles of my trainers. I gasp, "He's alive."

Noa catches up with me. "Another vision?"

I blink away rainwater. "I heard Vince." I look to the menacing sky. "Send as many storms as you want. It won't stop me finding him." I shudder and turn to Noa. "We're getting close. I know it."

Noa says nothing. He doesn't move. Water drips from his hair and forms tiny, glistening beads on his eyelashes.

I walk off, but Noa doesn't follow. I glance behind. "What's up?" My voice is sharp. "We can't miss this bus."

"You should let Edmonds know." He hesitates. "This might get dangerous."

"Vince's voice isn't enough. I need more." A bus approaches. "That's ours." I stick out my arm.

The bus brakes squeak and it judders to a stop, discharging exhaust fumes into the air, overwhelming the smell of wet ground. Doors jerk open and I step aboard.

After travelling for an hour, the bus rounds a corner and a sea of new housing development opens out. Beyond this, tower blocks clad in scaffolding loom over half-built apartment buildings. The foreground reminds me of a toy town, row upon row of identical terrace houses with tiny squares of garden breaking up the monotony of endless white walls. I'm on the edge of my seat, straining my neck left and right, because this all looks very similar to my vision.

I glance across to Noa. He's immersed in music; eyes closed, head back against the seat, fingers tapping against his knee.

I wipe condensation from the window to reveal a large green space surrounded by townhouses. *Shit. That's it.* I push past Noa and lunge for the bell, pressing it again and again.

"Steady on, love," shouts the driver.

My weight shifts from one foot to the other and I scream in my head for the bus to stop.

Noa's next to me, his headphones askew. He looks worried.

The brakes make a drawn-out creak, then the doors open and I jump out.

My heart pounds as my gaze wanders over the scene from the vision. The angular metal roofs of the terraced houses pierce the cloudy sky exactly like I visualised. *Where are you, Vince?*

"It reminds me of a Lowry painting, but without the factories and the smoke," says Noa. "The playground's at the far end." He pauses, then points to his right. "Luke's house is three rows back."

I walk along the path bordering the green space. Bronze and metal structures are interspersed with plants and narrow meandering trails lead to slides and swings. The squeals and laughter of children carry through the greenery.

On the swings sit two little boys in raincoats.

I stop. A lump forms in my throat. I sit opposite the boys on a damp wooden bench and watch them make arcs through the air.

I don't take my eyes off the boys. "Everything fits. Vince is *here*."

Noa sits beside me and taps my arm. "You should ring Edmonds." There's an edge to his voice. Maybe the connection with Luke is still preying on his mind?

"Okay." I hesitate. "Watch those boys like a hawk."

Noa gives a weak smile. "They don't look like criminal types."

I tilt my head. "You never know."

I walk to a quieter spot, away from the clamour of the playground and call Edmonds.

He's not impressed and says it's "nothing concrete," but he'll send a car round.

I hang up and sigh. If he's not going to take my visions seriously, why did he ask me to inform him?

Noa's still by the bench, staring into the distance.

His gaze tracks along the edge of the green space and he whispers into my ear, "A man wearing a skull ring just walked past. Sunglasses, plastic shopping bag."

I follow him to the path by the playground.

He nods. "Him."

A black-clad figure lopes along the path, his shoulders hunched so high, he's missing a neck. A plastic bag stretches into a taut band in his hand. Sharp corners tear through the white plastic. "Did the ring have ruby eyes?" I mutter, keeping my eyes on the man.

Noa's voice behind me, "Not sure." He pokes my shoulder. "You'd better call the cops again."

I bristle. "Edmonds wants *concrete* evidence. We don't know it's definitely him."

My heart thumps like it's going to burst from my chest. Keeping the man in my sights, I unbuckle my skateboard from my backpack and grasp it, ready to drop and go.

The handle of the man's bag snaps and cardboard cartons thud onto the path. He stuffs them back in and carries on walking with the bag wedged under one arm.

Noa clears his throat. "Luke's coming as back-up."

I turn and glare. "What?"

Noa levels with me. "That guy isn't Luke. This isn't your personal crusade. God knows what we're getting into here."

I turn back just as the man takes a corner. "Shit. We can't lose him." I pick up pace.

The man reaches the end of the street, then crosses towards a row of half-built semi-detached houses. One of the cartons falls to the ground.

I grab it as we pass. It's liquid breakfast and a chill goes through me. That stuff could keep someone alive for a while.

Noa's face is ashen. His gaze wanders up and down the street. "I don't like this, Marvel. No one lives around here." He stumbles over a sandbag weighing down a temporary fence.

Weeds sprout against incomplete walls and out of square, windowless holes. Uneven surfaces slow me down and drag my gaze to the ground instead of ahead. I don't like it here either. It's too isolated, and we're vulnerable.

Noa's arm swings out and hits me in the belly. "Quick, over here."

I follow him into a garage without a roof or door, and crouch down.

Noa peers around the block wall. "He went inside the end house." He texts into his phone.

The tendrils of a large weed hook into the concrete wall which borders us on three sides. Empty cement bags pile up in one corner, soggy and disintegrating into mush.

Footsteps pound towards me and a boy appears. The garage air fills with the smell of cheap body spray.

He slaps Noa on the back. "Alright, cuz. Been a while."

A hand waves in my face. "Luke. Good to meet you."

"Hi. I'm Marvel."

Luke squeezes my hand tight, then drops it. His angular face twitches and his eyes dart around the space and land on my skateboard. "Skater chick? Nice. You could take someone out with that." He stretches up onto the toes of his pristine white trainers and looks out of a rectangular hole high up on the outside wall, then hunkers down next to me and unzips a bag. Reaching inside, he pulls out a softball bat. "Got two bats, Mum's kitchen knife and pepper spray." He speaks fast and urgent.

I exchange a concerned glance with Noa.

Luke thrusts a softball bat into my hand.

It makes me nervous just holding it.

"Right, all armed-up. What's going down?" Luke kneels on the rough concrete floor and trains his eyes on the row of houses. His polyester sports shorts brush against my arm.

Noa fills him in.

"I last saw Vince three months ago," he says. "Edmonds grilled me, but I'm sweet. Took Mum to the movies that Friday." He looks from me to Noa. "Kidnapping's big league. Serious time if you get caught." Luke shakes his head. "Not worth it."

I catch Noa's eye and see relief.

The softball bat handle is moist with my sweat. "This is all too vigilante for me. I'll call Edmonds again."

Luke looks annoyed. "What did he say to you the first time?"

"He'd send a car round."

Luke sniggers. He peppers me with words like machine gun fire, "Yeah, so once they've helped a few old ladies cross the road, had a coffee, found a lost dog, filled in a ton of paperwork, then they might pitch up. Don't hold your breath. Cops like facts and right now you've got a random with a skull ring. He might be a homeless guy or a druggy or just taking a piss—God knows. I'm going over. Pass me that bat."

My mouth gapes open. I hand Luke the bat.

He springs up. "Watch my back." Luke races out and along the street with the softball bat slung over one shoulder.

I glance across to Noa. "Is he always like this?"

Noa sighs. "Yep. He's a Jackson Pollock."

I frown. "What do you mean?"

"Google his paintings. They're chaotic and explosive, filled with random splashes of colour." He hesitates. "Luke's got ADHD."

Unease swamps me and I've a sick feeling in my stomach. Luke's impulsiveness is a liability. "I'm calling Edmonds."

Noa grabs my arm. "Wait. He's coming back."

Luke's footsteps echo between the rows of houses. He squats next to me and talks between breaths. "Vince's in there. He doesn't look too hot." He snatches a breath and looks at me. "Call the cops and ambulance."

"The kidnapper. Did he see you?" Noa says.

"Don't think so." Luke looks down.

"You don't think so?" There's sarcasm in Noa's voice and a tense silence erupts between them.

If the kidnapper didn't see him, surely he must've heard him. I phone Edmonds.

I pull the phone away from my ear and address Luke. "Is the kidnapper armed?"

He stares at Noa and says in a cold voice, "No fucking idea." Luke stands and points a finger at Noa. "At least I've got the balls to go over. What use are you on crutches? You should've stayed home painting pictures of your old man."

Edmonds asks me what's going on. "It's fine—just get here fast." I hang up.

"And what do you do, Luke? Sell meth? Bet your mum's real proud."

Luke drops the bat and swings a punch at Noa who ducks out of the way.

"What the hell? Stop it." I step between them. A flutter of black catches my eye and I rush onto the street. "It's him."

I thrust a softball bat into Noa's hand. "I'll go to Vince." I meet Luke's dark eyes and he nods.

Luke grabs the other bat off the floor. "Don't worry. I'll get the bastard." He sprints, arms pumping and feet crunching over gravel, sending bits scuttling over the road.

Noa shouts after him, "Luke, wait."

Luke turns his head. "He'll be long gone by then."

Noa stuffs the other bat inside Luke's backpack, hurls the bag over his shoulder and swings his legs forward. He glances back at me.

The dispatcher's firing questions down the phone and all I can do is give Noa a thumbs up. Never thought I'd feel grateful about his crutches slowing him down.

I call Edmonds while I'm running to the house. Between breaths, I tell him the kidnapper scarpered and the boys are in pursuit. I sense restraint in his voice, like the lid on it's about to blow off. He asks again if the kidnapper's armed. "I don't know," I shout, and hang up.

The end house is more complete than the others. There's PVC windows and a roof but no cladding. White plastic wraps around it, blowing in and out with gusts of wind, like it's breathing. I run through the doorless entrance and into a space criss-crossed with stud walls. Discarded ends of timber and bent nails litter the floor. Smaller spaces feed off the main passageway and I poke my head into each one, bracing myself for what may lie within. Imagining what Luke meant by his description of Vince as *not too hot* conjures up all kinds of horrid thoughts. Has he been tortured? Is he covered in blood? Missing a few fingers? I push fear from my mind and forge on through the maze of vertical timber until I reach some concrete steps. *Vince has to be down here.* The steps lead to a cinder block garage and over in the far corner, surrounded by crushed liquid breakfast cartons, slumps Vince. He's not moving.

"Vince!" I rush over and shake his arm. He's floppy like a rag doll. I kick over a milk container full of piss. Its contents glug onto concrete floor, covering cartons and cigarette butts with a yellow glaze. The disgusting smell makes me gag.

I shake him harder and pinch his arm. "Vince, wake up. Please." My fingers push against his cool clammy neck for a pulse. It's faint and weak, like he's close to shutting down. His wrists and ankles are bound to the chair with black zip ties and they cut into his skin like cheese wire. Blood drips off the tips of his fingers and pools onto the floor below.

My heart pounds and my voice trembles. "Hold on, Vince." *What else can I do?* "Keep him warm," I mutter, as a pearl of first aid comes back to me. Then another: Resuscitation; thirty to two, compress mid chest, hundred beats a minute. *Shit, I hope it doesn't come to that.*

I take off my hoody and wrap it around him, then press his neck again. His chest rises and falls and I let out a long exhale as my fingers detect a pulse. I glance through the grimy window. "Where's the ambulance? Come on!"

Vince groans. A torrent of watery green vomit cascades onto the floor, splashing my shorts. "Ugh, gross." A sour smell engulfs the room and makes me retch again.

A faint siren in the distance grows louder. I sink to my knees and into a puddle of blood, vomit and piss.

Blue light flashes against the wall and a door slams. A man's voice hollers, "Hello there!"

My voice cracks. "In here. End house."

Paramedics swoop in, descending on Vince in a blur of blue surgical gloves and green uniforms. They cut off zip ties, stick small pads on his chest and attach him to beeping machines.

I step back and repeat to myself over and over again: *please don't die.* Sadie's words flood back to me about having faith in myself and her certainty about Shirley's prediction.

One of the paramedics brings in a collapsible stretcher and with deft, practised movement the two of them transfer Vince onto it. A transparent tube connects a needle in his arm to a bag of fluid held aloft and an oxygen mask fits over his nose and mouth. They cover him with a shiny silver blanket.

Finally, one of them turns to me. "Do you know him?"

I swallow. "He's my cousin."

"Okay. We'll do our best—he's very sick."

The paramedics push the stretcher through pools of urine and vomit, flattening cartons and bumping over loose fragments of timber.

Doors close. The ambulance roars away, its tyres flicking gravel against walls and its siren wailing into the wind.

My phone rings. It's Sadie.

"We found Vince. Cancel the auction." Talking is hard, like I can't get enough air, and my blood-stained fingers stick to the phone.

Sadie bombards me with questions, then starts to cry and asks if he'll die.

Emotion rises up and my lip quivers. "I don't know." My thoughts turn to Noa. "Sorry. I have to go." I hang up and run back to the garage to fetch my skateboard and backpack.

Through drizzling rain, I run towards smooth pavement and throw my board onto it, sending it rolling away. I chase after it and steady it with my foot, then pause; I've no idea where to go. I'm surrounded by rows of white-walled cookie-cutter homes, alleyways and roads. Noa doesn't answer my text. God, I stink. I take a right and hit a dead end. A woman with a dog approaches and I yell, "Where's the playground?"

She looks me up and down, then takes three slow steps back with her hands outstretched. The dog bares its teeth and growls. Ducking her head, she turns and scurries down an alleyway.

Great, now I'm scaring off the locals.

I skate beneath dull matt sky, along newly laid paths and follow my intuition.

I pop out of the end of an alleyway and before me is lush green open space, and people—lots of them. A crowd has gathered in the far right corner by a row of parked police cars and black SUVs. Police in body armour signal to them. An ambulance draws up. My heart lurches and I race over, slipping on wet grass and ploughing through prickly ornamental grasses. I search the crowd for Noa and Luke. There's no sign of them. People holler, jump out of my way and swear after me. Too breathless to shout at them to shift, I shove my way through. Police order everyone to move back, but I ignore their commands and continue to push against the tide of bodies coming the opposite way. Elbows meet mine and someone yells at me to turn around. I surge ahead, fuelled by the need to know if Noa and Luke are safe.

I stagger forward into open space, right myself and gasp. The kidnapper lies face down. Luke straddles him, twisting the kidnapper's arms up his back. Noa's standing to one side, a crutch rammed between the kidnapper's shoulder blades. I collapse onto my knees.

"Move back—*back*." A policeman pushes out with his hands. Handcuffs clink as he attaches them to the kidnapper's wrists. "Right lads, we'll take over now." He nods to Luke and Noa.

"Took your sweet time," says Luke. There are scratches across his face.

"Had to wait for armed response." The policeman helps the kidnapper stand.

Luke holds up a softball bat. "You already got armed response."

Edmonds steps forward. "And it's appreciated,

Luke. We have these procedures to ensure officers and the public are safe." He gives a weak smile. "Sports equipment is no match for a firearm. A cavalier attitude can get you killed. And he's not worth it." Edmonds sniffs and shoots the kidnapper a look of contempt.

Noa sees me and rushes over. "Marvel, what happened? You're covered in blood."

I stand up. "Oh, really?" No wonder that woman ran off.

"It's on your face, in your hair." His eyes wander over me, full of concern.

I feel faint and plunge to the ground.

Someone hands me a can of Coke and I gulp it down.

Noa's hand rests on my shoulder and Edmonds kneels next to me.

"Do you want me to call an ambulance?" asks Edmonds.

"No, I'll be okay." I realise I haven't eaten anything since leaving home. I drain the can and start to feel better.

"It's touch and go with Vince. They're trying to stabilise him." Edmonds sighs and looks chastened. "Sorry, Marvel. I should've taken your first call more seriously."

"I'm used to it. It's probably hard for you to understand how significant it was. I knew Vince was here." I look into the distance and shudder. Nothing I've achieved means anything if Vince dies.

"I'll need a statement off you later. I'll get an officer to drive you and Noa home." He hesitates. "We have an ID on the kidnapper. It's Alex Weston." Edmonds answers a phone call and raises a hand in farewell as he walks away.

I stare at Edmonds' back and remember Grant threatening to leave Vince for Alex back at the apartment. Did Alex and Grant hatch this plan together?

The crowd disperses and a group of teens part ways in front of me to reveal Luke hugging Noa. I ease myself up to standing and go over.

"Sorry about before. I didn't mean to have a go about your dad. Good you can draw. I wouldn't have the patience for any of that shit," says Luke, pulling away.

Noa looks down.

Luke continues. "I'm straight now. Starting a course soon, training to be an electrician."

Luke spots me and stares. "Woah. Who hit you?" His hands form fists and he paces towards the dispersing crowd. "Where is he?"

"It's Vince's blood," I say.

His face falls. "Sorry. I hope he makes it." He picks up his backpack and hurls it onto one shoulder, the weapons inside clunking against each other. "I'll be off."

Noa manages a smile. "Good to see you, Luke. Maybe you can come over soon and fix Mum's standing light."

Luke fist bumps him. "That'd be sweet." He nods to me, then turns and swaggers off across the grass.

I text Sadie. *Let me know as soon as you hear anything. Good or bad.*

I trudge after Noa, towards a waiting police car, and clench my blood-stained hands.

◆

Sleep isn't happening. I fling my tired body from one side of the bed to the other in restless agitation, constantly checking my phone for a message from Sadie. Moonlight seeps through the gaps in the curtains, but even this glimmer of light isn't enough to subdue the dark thoughts whirling through my mind. My ability to get a heads-up about the future is pointless if Vince dies and my purpose will evaporate like a puddle in searing Auckland sun. Knowing I tried my hardest to save him isn't enough.

A text beeps. I bolt upright and scrabble in the dark for my phone, knocking it off my bedside table and onto the floor. Cursing, I grope around for it and hold it against my chest. Before I read the message sent a minute after midnight, I look to the ceiling and pray to whatever deity is out there that Vince is alive.

He's stable. I'm going to hospital in morning x

I blow out a long exhale, ridding my lungs of yesterday's air.

I type back. *I'm coming with you.*

CHAPTER FOURTEEN

I hug Vince and beneath the scratchy cotton of his blue hospital gown, bony ribs press against mine. His thin frame looks lost within the hospital bed and a sheet hangs limply over his bent knees, its bleached whiteness matching the colour of his face.

Questions churn inside me, rising up then rolling back down again.

"Oh, my dear Vince, what an ordeal you've had." Sadie hugs him, then takes a step back. Her eyes wander over the tubes, bandages and transparent dressings fixed to Vince's body. She wobbles and grabs the metal bed frame to steady herself.

I pull up a chair for Sadie and perch on the end of the bed.

Vince looks at me. "My watch stopped in Flava. It reminded me of you."

"You realised I was right?" I say.

"Yes, but it was too late. I'm sorry." Vince's voice cracks. "Thanks for not giving up on me. You saved my life."

A lump forms in my throat and I can't speak. I reach forward and squeeze his hand tight.

Sadie rummages in her bag. "You read about people getting their drinks spiked in the papers. What a nasty piece of work that Alex was." She places a huge bag of grapes on the bedside table. "The charge nurse said you were lucky. Any longer and you might not have survived. You were dehydrated, hypothermic and withdrawing from drugs and alcohol." She chews a grape and swallows.

Vince's face turns a shade paler.

Sadie offers Vince a grape and says casually, "Has Grant been in?"

I grit my teeth.

"Briefly. He needed money." Vince manages a weak smile. "I didn't get paid last week, for obvious reasons." His eyes close, then flick open. "Sorry. I'm on Valium for alcohol detox. It knocks me out."

I pat his hand. "That's okay. We'd better get going and let you rest." I pause, then shuffle up the bed. My question niggles like a stitch in my side. "Can I ask you something?"

Vince nods.

"Did you see Alex's skull ring? It's the same as yours, isn't it?"

Vince presses a button on a remote control by his bed. There's a whirring sound and the head of the bed raises up. He screws up his eyes. "My memory's hazy. I'm not sure it was the same." He hesitates. "Grant says it's impossible. Mine's a unique design." He flops back onto a stack of pillows.

Why does everything Vince say create more questions? I frown. "Where is your r—"

Sadie shoots me a sharp look, then bends to kiss Vince. "The nurse said you'll be moved to the drug rehab unit tomorrow. We'll see you there." Sadie glances at me. "What time is Detective Edmonds meeting you?"

I sigh. "This afternoon."

Vince's eyelids flicker and he forces them open. He slurs, "Thanks for coming."

I give his hand one last squeeze.

In the lift, Sadie turns to me. "Are you still getting the vision of Shirley?"

"Yes, twice already this morning. Always the same. She's sat at the desk, writing."

"I wonder what she's telling you?" Her face creases with concentration. "It'll become obvious at some point. Just like all the others."

The joy of saving Vince was fleeting and there's a heaviness in my heart, like it's weighed down with sandbags from the building site where I found him. The visions led me to Vince and saved his life, just like Shirley predicted. But, Shirley's *still* on my case. I'm not making the mistake I made with the playground vision and spending weeks ignoring it. Figuring out why she's appearing to me is key, but my mind's a maze of dead-end streets and brick walls.

I slam the heel of my hand against the door opening sign on the lift panel and wait for Sadie to go first. A saying comes to me, one my dad uses all the time when he's investigating someone's murky past: *It's always the little things that catch people out.*

◆

Voices carry from the lounge. I hang up my hoody and walk in to find Edmonds sitting on the couch with a cup of tea.

Dad's regaling him with stories about his investigation into the Dark Web, stories I've heard a million times. In the background, on low volume, Dad's playing Supergrass's *Caught By the Fuzz*. Why is he so embarrassing?

"Marvel." Edmonds stands and shakes my hand. "How was Vince?"

"Pretty weak and skinny. Well, skinnier." I sit next to Edmonds and catch Dad's eye. "Did the reporters return?"

"Nope. Vince rescued. Baddie caught. Happy ending. Story arc complete." He clicks his tongue.

Edmonds grimaces. He clears his throat and meets my gaze. "I came to fill you in on the investigation and to thank you for your help." He straightens up. "Whilst we don't condone vigilante action, you and your friends were instrumental in finding Vince and capturing Alex Weston."

I bury my questions and force myself to listen.

"Weston pleaded guilty. He needed cash. He lost most of it investing in *Edge* and a property development company. The house where Vince was held was one of their developments. They went bust before it was finished."

I fold my arms across my chest. "The visions led me to Hobsonville Point and to Vince."

Edmonds gives a weak smile. "Yes. I realise that."

I wait for him to say more, but he avoids my eyes.

Dad raises his mug at me. "About bloody time something useful came from them, eh, Marvel?"

I shoot Dad a sharp look, then glance back to Edmonds, but he remains tight-lipped.

Edmonds takes a notebook from the inside pocket of his jacket and flicks through it. "Anyway. Weston travelled here from Australia on a false passport. Clearly, he wasn't intending to be caught." Edmonds tilts his head to me. "He denies having accomplices and unfortunately, we haven't been able to link anyone else to the crime." He closes his notebook.

I take a quick breath in. "Have you got Alex's skull ring? If it matches Vince's, then Grant's lying. And if he's lying about that, then—"

Edmonds frowns. "Alex wasn't wearing a skull ring when we brought him into custody."

"Noa saw it. Have you asked him?"

"Yes, he last saw Alex wearing it near the playground. It must have come off in the scuffle. No big deal. It doesn't prove anything."

I look down and let out a long sigh. *No big deal?*

Dad returns after showing Edmonds out. He stares ahead with a confused look on his face. "He doesn't have the private key."

"What are you on about?"

Dad turns to me. "Weston claims the ransom bitcoin address is his. Edmonds liaised with the cops in Australia, got his computer seized. Nothing." He mumbles, "Though he may have used a foreign VPN, but still …"

"Dad! I have no idea what you mean."

"If Weston doesn't have the private key to his own bitcoin wallet, it means he doesn't own it."

"Then Edmonds needs to find out who does."

Dad sighs. "And therein lies the problem. Bitcoin addresses are virtually untraceable."

◆

Lying on my bed, I take slow deep breaths and try to order my thoughts. How can Edmonds be so relaxed? Surely he wants justice for Vince and the accomplices caught? The skull ring dominates my thoughts. I'm certain Alex and Vince's skull rings are identical, but why won't Grant admit it? Is there something about the rings he doesn't want discovered?

I bolt upright and Google the drug rehab unit. It's a twenty-minute walk.

A text pings. It's Noa. A warm feeling sweeps through me. *I have Sunday off. Want to meet up?*

I push back visiting Vince until after lunch and type back: *Eleven? Usual place?*

He signs off with a happy face emoji and my day brightens like the sight of an empty skate park where I'm free to ride ramps and grind rails as many times as I please.

CHAPTER FIFTEEN

I yank my curtains open. The crack in the window brings my worries flooding back and questions zip through my mind. I think of Sadie's words about Shirley's vision and push my fingers against my temples. *It'll become obvious at some point. Just like all the others.*

Dad's in the lounge typing furiously into his laptop. His faded Cure T-shirt features a young Robert Smith, his back-combed hair defying gravity.

He glances up. "Fresh coffee on the bench. Can't talk, got to finish this."

I pour myself a cup and listen to the frantic tapping of Dad's fingers and near constant run of expletives, the hallmark of Dad under pressure.

He looks up at me. "Done. May as well cash in while I can. A thousand words on false passports. Link it to my Dark Web article and bingo—more subscribers to my blog, more freelance work."

I give a wry smile and look at his shirt. "And more lame T-shirts."

Dad rubs his hands together. "Oh, yes."

I lift the mug to my lips, then pause. "What's the connection between false passports and the Dark Web?"

He shakes his head. "I told you before, Marvel, you can buy anything on there. *Anything.*"

Mum drags in a painting wrapped in layers of bubble wrap. "Simon, can you keep an ear out for the courier?" She runs her hand across the packaging. "Farewell, *Disturbance of a Daughter's Dreams.*" She turns to me. "You're looking so much better. Good you slept in."

"Yes." I force a smile. "My dreams are no longer disturbed." Only my waking hours torment me now.

I change the subject. "I'm off to see Vince later on. The rehab place is just up the road."

Dad shifts in his chair. "Right, yes. I should probably pay him a visit. Tell him to follow me on Spotify. I've compiled him a classic Simon Harris playlist."

"Thanks, Dad." I drain my coffee. "Right, got to meet Noa."

Mum tapes a label onto the package. "How long until he's off those crutches?"

I exhale. "Nearly three weeks done, another three to go."

"Great. Let me know if there's any news about art school."

I cross my fingers. "Yep."

The street is quiet and my heart leaps. I charge down the pavement and onto the road, hurtling towards a speed bump. The skateboard lifts and I'm weightless for a second, before crashing back onto asphalt. My focus shifts to pulling off the perfect S-shape. Nothing else matters as I curve downhill and sweep across the road through dappled sunlight, adjusting my bodyweight to create the turn.

I wait by the pedestrian crossing at the main intersection of Taylor's Hill, wedging my skateboard under one arm. Next to me are two familiar boys. "Hi, Tavita. Hi, Isaia."

"Hey, Marvel," says Isaia. "Want a chip?" He tilts his head towards his older brother, who's holding a paper cone of hot chips.

Tavita shovels a handful into his mouth, then offers me one.

I smile. "No, thanks."

The boys' lips are slick with grease and their hands wave over their mouths, cooling down the hot morsels.

The light change is taking ages. I hop from one foot to the other, like a jogger frustrated with losing time.

A sudden gust of cold air displaces the sun's warmth and a feeling of dread comes over me.

The two boys laugh, unaware their feet are edging closer to the road.

The smell of car exhaust fumes drifts past. Tyres

screech. A vision of blurry black metal and silver wheels flashes up. I look around for a speeding car, but there isn't one.

The green man signal starts and Noa's brothers cross.

I realise just in time and throw out my left arm, thrusting the boys backwards. Chips fly to the ground like overweight confetti.

"Hey, what are you doing?" yells Isaia, pushing my arm away.

A car appears from the side street, tears around the corner and through the red light. Chips flatten onto asphalt, leaving a tyre-tracked veneer of potato over the road.

The hot blast of exhaust fumes makes the boys cough and through red, watery eyes they stare at me.

"You knew?" says Tavita, holding what's left of his chips.

I hesitate. "Yes. I saw it happen a few seconds before."

Their mouths gape open and a look of amazement passes between them.

Tavita's eyes widen. "Wow, you're like a guardian angel. That car would've killed us both."

I shake my head. "Yeah. Red light runners are the worst."

◆

Noa's beaten me to the park bench again. His crutches rest against the wooden arm and his dark curls are like small coiled springs, stretching then recoiling as his head bobs to music.

"Hey, Marvel." He pulls down his headphones. "Great news about Vince."

"Yes. It is." I huddle in next to him and smell freshly laundered clothes. "I just saw your brothers at the lights."

"Were they behaving?"

I pause. "Yep, they were just fine."

Noa fumbles in his pocket. "Here, I thought you should have this as a memento." He places the skull ring in my palm.

I gasp. "Wow. How did you get it?" Sparkling ruby eyes meet mine and I run my finger over the contours of the skull markings, perfectly engraved into the silver. Without a shade of doubt, it's the ring from my vision. I turn to Noa. "Did it slip off Alex's finger?"

Noa screws up his face. "Well, Luke kind of pulled it off. He wanted to sell it on Trade Me."

I roll my eyes. "How did you persuade him to part with it?"

Noa hesitates. "I told him the ring led you to Vince and you should be the one to keep it." He looks down. "Do you think I should come clean to Edmonds?"

I close my hand tight around the ring. "Nah. He said the ring is no big deal and doesn't prove anything."

Noa hesitates and searches my face. "Do *you* think it's important?"

"I'm not sure." I open my palm. "What do you

think that is?" I point to the letters M.A inscribed on the inside of the ring, next to the hallmark.

Noa cranes forward. "The maker's own mark?"

I meet his eyes. "Yes. So it's not mass-produced. But is it unique?"

"Why does it matter?"

"I'm trying to work that out."

Noa's face falls. "Don't do this again. If you know something, tell me. You promised."

"All I know is Grant denies he bought Alex and Vince matching rings and I believe that's a lie."

Noa stands and winces. "I can't. I've got to go to the hospital."

Guilt floods over me. *Did he hurt himself chasing after Alex?* "Is everything alright?"

"Don't know. My ankle's pretty sore after yesterday. I rang the ward and they told me to come in for a check-up." He leans onto the crutches. "Taxi's on its way."

By the time we get to the main road, sweat is trickling down Noa's forehead and I wipe his brow with the sleeve of my hoody. "I'll come with you. I can visit Vince later."

"No. You should go. He needs his family." The word, family, causes Noa to choke up and he slaps away a tear.

I grab his arms. "Are you upset with me? Honestly, Noa, once I know something I won't keep it from you."

He shakes his head. "It's not you. I'm just having a rough day. Sorry."

A taxi pulls up alongside Noa and I open the passenger door. "I'll text you later."

The second the taxi pulls away, I regret not getting in. It's like my heart is at the centre of a tug-of-war contest between equally matched teams. I watch Noa's taxi until it merges onto the motorway on-ramp, heading towards the city.

◆

Vince is waiting for me in the visitor's room. He's on the couch, dabbing his eye with a tissue.

I hesitate on the threshold, then walk over and hug him. "Good to see you."

He sniffs and wipes away tears. Shreds of white tissue fall onto the carpet.

I sit on the couch opposite and my gaze wanders to the courtyard outside, where a picnic table is surrounded by palms, flax and small glossy-leaved shrubs. I clear my throat. "Dad's made you a playlist. You just need to follow him on Spotify."

Vince clasps his shaking hands together. "Thanks." His eyes dart around the room unable to settle, and his forehead glistens with sweat.

Questions bubble up and I bite my lip.

I reach across and place a hand on his. "You're going to get better."

He shakes his head. "Sorry. I'm not much company." He meets my eyes. "Grant's ended it with me."

I pull my hand back and dig my fingers into the grubby seat cushion. "I'm sorry. That's the worst timing." I block the anger in my voice. "When did he drop that bombshell?"

"Earlier. He brought in what's left of my stuff. He sold anything valuable." Vince gives a watery smile. "Guess I'm no use to him now I'm in recovery." He looks down.

"What do you mean?"

More tears roll down Vince's cheeks. "I had no idea he'd defaulted on the mortgage and wasn't paying the bills. I was too out of it to notice what was going on with my money, but now I realise Grant was living off me."

A thought strikes me and I pitch forward. "What's happened to your skull ring and the box of your mum's stuff?"

Vince shrugs. "Might still be at the apartment. He's probably flogged the ring by now. The journals were full of weird sketches, they didn't mean anything. No big loss." He wrestles out words like the effort saps all his energy.

No. I need that ring. I cover my face.

Vince talks through sobs. "I miss him. Grant wasn't perfect, but he was always thoughtful. After my dealer left me in the lurch, Grant had drugs mailed to the apartment every week. That's how caring he was."

Irritation pricks me. "You know it was your ex-dealer, Luke Salesa, who caught Alex Weston." I feel a twinge of guilt. "Err, and my friend, Noa."

He looks surprised. "Oh."

"The three of us took massive risks for you." I remember Noa's painful leg and cringe.

Vince takes a ragged inhale.

A knock on the door and a soft female voice. "Counselling in five minutes."

Vince projects to the door. "Okay. Thanks."

"You're part of our family and we want you back." I stand up. "Did you know Grant asked Sadie for the ransom money? She said that's only the second time he's visited. The first was to ask for investment in *Edge* magazine."

Vince frowns and looks down.

Grant's not who you think he is, Vince. And I'm going to prove it.

I place a hand on the door handle. "Hang in there. See you soon."

Vince smiles weakly. "Thanks, Marvel."

Music drifts from one of the rooms along the corridor. The tune reminds me of a song Dad plays. I slap my hand against my forehead; Dad, resident expert in subterfuge and dirty tricks, is just the person I need.

CHAPTER SIXTEEN

On the way home, I stop and text Noa: *How did it go at the hospital? Remember I promised to tell you stuff? Can you be at mine in ten mins?*

Shirley's vision returns as I'm turning the key in the door. I screw up my eyes and rest my forehead against peeling paintwork.

A car rumbles behind me and comes to a standstill.

Noa gets out. "Thanks." He carefully adjusts his crutches, then looks up. "Hi."

The car reverses down the driveway and tense silence erupts in the space between us.

"Are you alright?" I say.

Noa's face falls. "The doctor told me to be careful. The bone's not knitting together as fast as she'd like."

Guilt stings me. "It never crossed my mind you might not get better."

He smiles weakly. "Well, you've had a lot on your mind."

"Sorry."

"Stop apologising. You just prevented my brothers getting run over."

My face burns. "Oh, God." I hesitate. "They didn't tell your mum, did they?"

"No. A neighbour saw it happen and told her." Noa raises his eyebrows and waits.

"I didn't think you needed to know," I mumble. "It's kind of embarrassing."

Noa's crutches creak and he propels towards the front door. "You saved their lives. There's nothing embarrassing about that."

Inside, Dad's snoring in the armchair. His belly wobbles on the exhale and a roll of pink flesh pokes out beneath his T-shirt, overhanging his belt. I usher Noa towards the couch and push the ottoman closer to his legs.

Before I wake Dad, I prepare the scene. No way can I afford to lose two hours if he's in a grump. I make him a cup of tea, then press play on his favourite John Coltrane CD and hope for the best.

I pass Noa a mug of tea. "Okay. Let's wake Sleeping Beauty."

I shake Dad's shoulders and whisper in his ear, "Dad, I made you a nice cup of tea."

He groans and opens one eye. "Oh, right. What time is it?"

"Almost five."

He depresses a lever and the back of the chair jolts forwards. "Oh, hello, Noa. How's that leg?"

I grimace.

"Yeah, not bad. I need to rest it more," he says.

Dad takes a sip and tilts his head to me. "Well, life's never restful with Marvel, always some supernatural shit going down."

Noa holds my gaze and smiles. "Yep."

Lines of questions form on the tip of my tongue and I shuffle my feet against the carpet, waiting for Dad to finish his tea.

He places his empty mug on the coffee table and that's my cue.

"Grant bought Vince drugs. They arrived packaged up in the mail. Do you think he bought them off the Dark Web? With bitcoin?"

Dad shrugs. "Probably."

I perch on the edge of the couch. "I need to understand how bitcoin works. Can they link the ransom bitcoin address to anyone?"

Dad sighs. "Police already checked it out. Multiple small payments and a larger payment about two weeks ago. Edmonds told me their experts tracked the small payments to the Dark Web, but that's as far as it goes. They can't pinpoint the vendor or the buyer. Whoever is behind this knows their shit. They'll have used TOR and an overseas VPN, so browsing the Dark Web won't link to an IP address."

It's like he's talking a foreign language. "So, Edmonds knows about Grant buying Vince drugs?"

"It's alleged. Grant denies it and it's impossible to prove."

Noa and I exchange a confused glance.

I press my fingers to my temples. "Okay. Pretend Noa and I have never heard of bitcoin. Tell us the basics as *simply* as possible."

Dad leans back in his chair. "I'll need another cup of tea, then. Two sugars."

I hand Dad his favourite mug, the one with the word *Legend* printed on it. Steam rolls off the hot tea and spirals through the air.

He slurps a mouthful and gives me an approving nod. "Okay." He inhales deeply. "There's a few ways the owner of a bitcoin address can be discovered. One: use a bitcoin exchange, which by law has to record users' details, to exchange bitcoin for cash and police subpoena the records. Two: an undercover cop masquerades as a Dark Web vendor to obtain the site's buyers' personal details; or three, open source intelligence sources like Twitter can link a public bitcoin address to a person's name or email—sounds daft but you'd be surprised how dumb people can be."

Noa looks blank. "You lost me before, at TOR and VPN."

Dad flicks his eyes to the ceiling. "TOR stands for The Onion Router. It enables anonymous communication across the Internet. By also using a logless VPN—virtual private network—there's no way of linking your home computer to dodgy places like the Dark Web."

I lock eyes with Dad. "You always talk about little things catching people out."

Dad smiles. "I most certainly do. But, in this case it really is a needle in a haystack situation."

A thought strikes me. "One of those Dark Web transactions could have been for Alex's false passport?"

"Possible, but not provable."

He forgets I deal with the unprovable on a regular basis. "I'm phoning Edmonds."

Dad frowns. "Why? I told you everything he told me."

"I have a few questions."

Dad mutters something under his breath. "Police have moved on. Studying bitcoin transactions is time consuming—there's only so much time and money." He stands and stretches. "Good luck." He gives Noa a thumbs up. "Catch you later, mate."

Dad wanders back to his study.

Noa grits his teeth. "I need to move. My leg's seizing up." He cradles his leg with both hands and lifts it off the ottoman. He looks up. "What's bothering you?"

I tug at a loose thread of denim and snap it off. "Grant's part of the kidnapping plot. I'm going to find that weak link if it kills me."

I dial Edmonds. He answers after the third ring, says a gruff hello, then barks instructions to someone.

"Hi, it's Marvel. About the bitcoin. That large bitcoin payment was to Weston, right? Hush money? Payment for the kidnapping?"

He lectures me about supposition and rattles off his usual line about lack of evidence. Apparently, he's dealing with more pressing cases now and he's done his best with limited resources. All in all, he says it was a good outcome.

My hand tightens around the phone. "A good outcome? Vince almost died. Someone paid Weston to do it on condition he didn't rat out his accomplices. And you're happy with that?"

Edmonds voice hardens. He chides me for wasting police time and hangs up.

I sink my head. "The case is closed." I look up. "I have to uncover the truth. I owe it to Vince." My hands form fists. "I want him to see what I see when I look at Grant."

Noa's gaze wanders to Mum's paintings hanging on the wall. "If 'saving your cousin' was a painting, would the artist be me or your mum?" He turns to me. "And who would be the subject?"

I stare at Noa. *What is he on about? What has any of this got to do with art?*

He smiles. "It doesn't matter." He grabs his crutches and hauls himself up. "Mum asked if you'd like to come over for dinner tomorrow night as a thank you for saving the boys."

A warm feeling rolls through me. "Thanks, I'd like

that." I look at the moon boot protecting his lower leg and swallow. "I'll phone you a taxi."

◆

I lie on my bed. My mind's a whirl of bitcoin transactions shunting back and forth across the Blockchain. I think of Edmonds and try to conjure facts, but nothing implicates Grant. All I have is my own conviction. Edmonds is right. I am making assumptions, bending the facts to suit my own agenda. As far as the police are concerned, the culprit's behind bars and there's a big fat tick in the case closed box.

I think about Noa's ankle and shudder. Racing to catch the bus to Hobsonville Point and chasing after Alex have messed up his recovery. And he did this to help me. I can't give up now.

I stare at the ceiling and it dawns on me I'm going about this the wrong way. Concentrating on "cold, hard facts" will get me nowhere. Being psychic *is* useful. Visions led me to Alex, then to Vince. Instead of thinking like a cop, I need to think like a psychic.

I focus on *my* facts. The skull ring from my vision matches Alex's and Vince's. Then why won't Grant admit buying Alex's ring? And how could he afford to buy Vince one if he couldn't even pay his mortgage? A memory flashes up of unopened mail strewn over the hall table in Grant's apartment. The words *Final Demand* stamped in red ink on the envelopes. I whack my hand against the wall. Of course. Grant's lying about the skull ring to cover his tracks.

I sit up. Finding Vince's ring is crucial. Goosebumps prickle along my arms at the thought of facing Grant again. My hands ball into fists and I hammer them against the bed. Not only am I too chicken to go alone, but bringing Noa is no defence against Grant. It's foolhardy and I'm probably breaking the law, but I have no choice: Luke's a loose cannon and I need his help.

CHAPTER SEVENTEEN

The first day back at school drags. Every lesson passes in a slow blur as my mind dwells on retrieving Vince's ring and my dread of visiting Grant.

Back home, I change into my best white T-shirt and the only pair of jeans I own that aren't ripped, and head to Noa's, aiming to get there for six.

I skate around a bend, rolling over sections of lit and unlit road, through patches of darkness, then back into light streaming from houses and streetlights. My front wheel grinds against something and stops, sending me sprawling onto the road. My skateboard whacks into the tyre of a parked car and I throw the pebble that locked my wheel into a shrub. Memories of bullies chucking stones in my path tumble back. Their ringing laughter as I crawled, bleeding, to the kerb. I dust myself down and wipe bits of gravel from my stinging palms. Fraying strands of denim hang from new rips over each knee and my grazed skin burns.

I shove my skateboard under my arm and walk the rest of the way.

Turning the corner into Noa's street, unease washes over me. I whisper to the ground, "Don't be stupid, it's only a dinner."

By the time I reach Noa's driveway, foreboding hovers over me like a raincloud in a windless sky. My skateboard slips from my grip and rolls, splashing into a rain-filled pothole. The weeds in Noa's front yard glow in the light from steamed-up windows and the smell of roasting meat wafts towards me. I stop. Shirley's vision flashes up. All that woman does is write. She's getting pissed off with me about something, because three appearances in one day must be a record. How many of those old school journals did she get through? I crouch down and fish my filthy skateboard out of the black water. Vince's words repeat in my mind: *The journals were full of weird sketches, they didn't mean anything.* I straighten up slowly like unwinding a new piece of grip tape. *Maybe they just didn't mean anything to you, Vince.*

I stride up Noa's driveway and ring the doorbell.

Teuila opens the door, her slender arm stretching out to reach the lock. Her smile falls as she clocks my bloody knees. "Ooh, Marvel. They look sore." She turns to Noa who's behind her.

I stash my skateboard against the wall and step

into the warm hallway. "Yeah, I had an altercation with a pebble."

Noa grins. "Come through. I'll go find a couple of plasters."

The metal clang of a pot lid carries from the kitchen and an oven door slams.

Teuila grips my arm and tugs me along the hallway and into the lounge.

Noa's brothers play-fight on the couch, stopping when they see me.

"Hi, boys," I say.

They mumble a greeting and shuffle apart, guilty looks on their faces.

Teuila sticks her nose in the air and leads me to the opposite couch. She huddles so close, our arms touch. She shields her mouth with one hand and whispers, "Do you want to know a secret?" Before I can reply, she blurts, "Noa's doing a portrait of you. I crept into the shed and saw it." Glancing briefly to the door, she turns back to me. "And it really looks like you, too."

The surprise in her voice makes me smile.

She squeezes my hand. "Don't tell him. He'll be mad."

"I won't. It can be our little secret."

Teuila's face brightens. She hugs me, enclosing my waist with her arms like a belt pulled too tight.

Luisa appears carrying a tray of food and sets it down on the coffee table. "Hi, Marvel." Her face is red and a sheen of sweat glistens across her forehead.

"Good evening, my dear," Emmeline booms, laying another tray on the table. She walks over to me with wide outstretched arms. "Thank you for protecting my sons."

I spring up and she squeezes me in a bear hug, swamping my senses with cooking smells and the scent of jasmine.

She releases me and grips my shoulders. "You are too skinny. Does your mother not feed you?" She reaches over to the coffee table and thrusts a plate into my hand. "Here, you must eat." She points to each dish in turn. "Roast chicken, cassava, corned beef and coconut rice."

"Thank you. It looks great." Luisa, Tavita and Isaia each have a plate balanced on their lap and on the white wall above them hangs a simple wooden crucifix. I overfill my plate and catch the satisfied look on Emmeline's face.

Noa appears holding a small box of Band Aids and sits next to me. "Sorry, they weren't in their usual place."

Manoeuvring around my plate, I stick plasters to my knees and nearly send my plate flying with the shock of Emmeline's thunderous clap. *What the hell?*

Noa and his siblings bow their heads while she says a prayer.

"Amen," says everyone, apart from me. Cutlery chimes and the younger children descend on the table of food, arms reaching across it, forming a spider-web of limbs.

Emmeline sits like a queen, knees together, shoulders back, in an armchair raised higher than the couches. "Honestly, those boys." She raises her eyes at Tavita and Isaia. "They make up such silly stories about you, say you can see the future." She tuts.

I swallow. The room falls quiet, disturbed only by munching and the scrape of a knife against a plate.

Noa glares at his two brothers, who sink their heads. He whispers to me, "I'm sorry."

My grip on the cutlery tightens and I lock eyes with Emmeline. "Sometimes, I do see the future."

Emmeline stops chewing. "Oh."

Noa takes a sharp inhale.

"See, told you, Mum," says Isaia in a wounded voice.

Noa taps his knife on the rim of his plate to get Isaia's attention, then puts a finger to his lips. "The kidnapped hairdresser was Marvel's cousin. She had a vision of the place where he was being held and found him."

Emmeline's face clouds over. "It's against our beliefs. You should put your faith in Divine Providence." She glances to the crucifix on the wall.

Hot anger rises up and I level with Emmeline. "If I'd done that, then Vince, Isaia and Tavita would be dead."

Isaia gasps and looks across at Tavita.

Noa straightens up. "Marvel can't help it. These visions come to her, she doesn't seek them out."

Emmeline slaps the chair arm. "Then you should ignore them."

"I tried that. And look what happened." I point to Noa's leg.

Her voice hardens. "You did the right thing, then. Only God can reveal the future."

Noa squeezes my arm. "Sorry, Mum. We'll have to agree to disagree."

Emmeline's mouth forms a wary smile. "You should know better, Noa. You've been raised in the Church."

My appetite drains. I force myself to finish the rest of the food, but my mouth is dry and every bite takes forever to chew.

Teuila sniffs and wipes away a tear.

Noa takes my plate and excuses us both.

I thank Emmeline.

She looks at the threadbare carpet and mutters a stiff goodbye.

The children give limp waves, their silence hanging in the air like a popped party balloon.

Noa joins me at the end of the driveway. "I'm sorry. My brothers messed up. Mum's pretty staunch."

I look at the ground and hold back tears. "Maybe I shouldn't have told her the truth."

"She'd have found out at some point."

My face goes hot and I'm grateful for the darkness. "Do you think she'll accept me?"

Noa's eyes shine beneath a streetlight. He hesitates. "I don't know." He moves closer. "You can't give up because of her. Keep going. Remember you're Kandinsky."

I shake my head. "Who?"

Noa smiles. "He was the pioneer of abstract art. Obsessed with the spiritual and the human soul."

"Was he any good?"

Noa laughs, then stops and looks at me. "He was amazing."

I distract myself from his gaze and brush crumbs off my T-shirt, then change the subject. "I need a big favour."

I ask if he'll come with me to visit Grant after school tomorrow. "I desperately need Vince's ring and his mother's journals. I think I can prove Grant's behind the kidnapping." I pause. "We'll need Luke."

Noa's eyes widen. "Is Grant violent?"

"I don't know."

Noa hesitates. "You really think you're onto something here?"

Doubt bubbles up and I push it from my mind. "Yes."

He raises one crutch. "I'll talk to Luke."

I exhale. "Thanks." A sudden panic engulfs me and I clutch Noa's arms. "Do you think your mum will ask you not to see me again?"

"No, course not." There's uncertainty in his voice. "I'm eighteen. I choose my own friends." He leans forward and kisses my lips. "We'll just keep the psychic stuff under wraps from now on."

Hot emotion churns through me. *I thought we were just friends? Why is my life so complicated?* And now he's siding with me against his mum. My heart screams at me to hold on tight. Noa is too good to lose.

The skate home calms my overthinking brain. "Get a grip," I mutter to myself. *Stay focused.*

Noa texts: *Luke's a goer.* I smile. Of course he is.

Closer to home, doubt creeps in again and cold dread spikes me at the thought of facing Grant. Bright stars in the sky capture my attention and hope surges through me, crushing my negativity. *Have faith.*

I accelerate towards the speed bump and nail the landing. Tomorrow will bring me another step closer to justice.

CHAPTER EIGHTEEN

Ponsonby Road traffic whizzes past and coffee aromas drift across the pavement. Alex's skull ring clinks against loose change in my jeans pocket and Noa's crutches click beside me as he swings forward. In the distance, Luke's sitting on a bench with an arm outstretched along the top like he owns it.

He raises a finger in greeting as we approach. His bulging backpack rests by his feet and a bolt of anxiety shoots through me. Hoping Luke won't do anything crazy is like trusting no one will nick your brand new skateboard from outside a dairy.

Luke stands and slaps Noa's back. "How's it going?" He nods to me, then claps his hands. "Right, where's it at?"

I point down Picton Street. "This way."

Luke hauls his backpack onto one shoulder and zips up his tracksuit top. "So, what's this Grant fella done?"

"Nothing I can prove." I pause. "But I'm working on it."

The pretty tree-lined street before me is flanked by stately weatherboard villas. It's not the street's fault, but being the quickest route to Grant's apartment has tarnished it forever.

Luke's a few steps ahead. He looks back. "Why do you even need me?"

I tell him Grant has some of Vince's valuables and we need to retrieve them before the bank takes the apartment.

Outside the 1960s apartment block, I press a shaky finger against the buzzer.

"Hello?" Grant's voice sends a shiver down my spine.

"It's Marvel Harris, Vince's cousin. He asked me to collect a box of his mum's stuff. It wasn't with the rest."

Luke rolls his eyes. "A box of his mum's stuff? I could've stayed in bed."

Noa glares at Luke and points to the intercom transmitting Grant's raspy breathing.

A loud buzz makes me jump and the door clicks open.

Luke pushes hard against it and sighs. "Don't know why I bothered."

Grant's apartment door is wedged open with an ornamental bronze skull. Speed Metal rages from the lounge, surging towards us through a hallway crammed with cardboard boxes.

Luke lifts the skull and weighs it in both hands. "Solid. Might get a hundy for it."

Noa shoots him a sharp look.

"Hi," I shout down the hall and feel the hairs on the back of my neck rise. My stomach tightens at the smell of Grant's woody aftershave.

The music dies down. Grant appears carrying a box and drops it at my feet. A gust of air ripples the frayed hem of my jeans. "There you go, sweetheart. You can bugger off now." He looks at the boys and sniggers. "Who are these two, your bodyguards?"

Grant's dark oppressive energy eclipses me and I battle against it, forcing myself not to step away. The edges of his aura splinter into grey and black segments, like arms reaching out to drag me further into his dark orbit. My voice trembles. "Vince would like his skull ring back, too."

Grant sneers. "I don't have it."

Luke bends and unzips his backpack. He steps forward, holding a softball bat over his shoulder. "Stop pissing about and give her the ring."

Grant sticks his face close to Luke's. "Don't threaten me." He takes out his phone. "Get out or I'm calling the police."

I throw an arm in front of Luke. "Go right ahead. And I'll prove to them you bought Vince drugs off the Dark Web." My heart rate ratchets up. I've always been a crap liar.

Grant narrows his eyes and steps back. "Bullshit. Nothing links to me."

"Give us the ring and we'll be out of here," Luke says.

Grant's gaze wanders over Luke's pristine white trainers, baggy black shorts and back-to-front baseball cap. "I pawned it, sweetie."

Luke lowers the softball bat. "Which branch of Cash Converters?"

Grant prods Luke's chest. "Short *and* stupid are we? Do I look like the kind of guy who pawns low-end shit?"

Luke swings the softball bat.

Noa grabs it mid-air and one of his crutches thuds onto carpet. "Luke, leave it."

I pick up Noa's crutch, then reach back down for the box and meet Grant's beady eyes. "Vince is *so* much better off without you."

Grant smirks. "Give my regards to your dear grandmother." He kicks the bronze skull and the door closes, driving us back.

In the stairwell, I crouch down and wait for my heart rate to settle. Waves of anger roll over me as the conversation plays back in my head. The bastard's sold it. *What am I going to do now?* My case against Grant hinges on finding that ring.

"What a freak," says Luke. He shoves the softball bat into his backpack. "All those black walls gave me the heebies."

Noa stares at the closed apartment door. "What did your cousin see in him?" He turns to me. "What was he thinking?"

"He wasn't thinking. He was addicted to drugs and

alcohol." Reaching out to push an errant curl from Noa's face, I stop and scratch my face instead.

"Yeah, Vince was one of my regulars." Luke adjusts his baseball cap. "Dark Web's cheaper, but all it takes is some smart-arse customs officer to open your parcel and bang." He punches his fist into his palm.

I hand Luke the box and hold one of Noa's crutches, allowing him to grip the banister and manoeuvre down the stairs. "Take it easy on that ankle."

In the hallway below, Luke paces backwards and forwards, scratching the cardboard box with his fingers. "How badly do you want this ring? It's probably in one of the pawn shops in town; they're the nearest and they have shitloads of jewellery."

"I have to find it." My words echo off the stairwell walls.

Luke blows out air and continues to pace. "It'll cost you."

I stop dead, knowing my bank balance comes to about fifty bucks. *Shit*.

Noa balances on one leg, having run out of banister. "Marvel, I need that."

Guilt blasts away money worries and I rush down the stairs, handing him the other crutch. "Sorry."

Noa glances from me to Luke. "Right, what now?"

The boys exchange a look.

I snap, "No point thinking about money until we find the ring." Dollar signs parade through my mind, teasing me about the major flaw in my plan.

Balancing the box on his head, Luke takes a selfie. *Why does he have to be such a dick?*

Noa cracks up.

"Luke! Where are the pawn shops?" I sigh, wishing I was as clued up as him about the shonky underside of Auckland life.

He throws Shirley's box in the air and snatches it back. "Follow the rich and the desperate. Where does it take you?"

I'm in no mood for riddles either. "No idea." I shove past him and elbow the door release.

"The casino." He follows me out. "Man, you two need to get out more."

I turn around to face Luke. "Promise me you'll keep that bat in your bag from now on."

Luke shrugs. "Yeah, alright. Whatever."

◆

Luke swaggers up Victoria Street holding Shirley's box with one hand, like a posh waiter carrying a tray. Up ahead, the Sky Tower pierces into grey cloud and at its base squats the casino.

Noa's pace is slow. "Sore arms," he says, looking across to me.

"You should go back. The bus stop's just up there." Mixed feelings churn. "Remember what the doctor said."

"I'm staying with you." His eyes shift to the dairy on his right. "I'll grab a Coke."

"Wait here." Racing into the dairy, I shout back, "Keep your eye on Luke."

Pressing the cold can into Noa's hand, I glance up the hill.

Luke's pacing outside a shop front, shunting the cardboard box from one arm to the other. He spots me and bats his palm forward, mouthing the words, *hurry up*.

The pawn shop's next to an Indian takeaway. Strong curry smells hit me and my stomach grumbles. Ignoring thoughts of food, I march into the pawn shop and face a wall of designer handbags.

A harsh voice. "Can I help you?" The shop assistant appraises each one of us in turn and the scowl on her chubby face deepens.

In glass cabinets below me are rows of watches and jewellery. Hot light heats the back of my neck as I scrabble around in my jeans pocket and pull out Alex's ring. "I'm looking for a ring like this."

The shop assistant examines the ring with a magnifying glass, then hands it back to me. Her voice softens. "It's white gold and ruby. I can give you a thousand dollars." There's a glimmer in her eyes. "You're over eighteen, right?"

I pocket the ring. "It's not for sale. Like I said, I'm looking for one similar."

The woman taps a pink varnished fingernail on the glass. "All our rings are in here."

There's no skull ring in the cabinet.

I look up. "Have you sold a ring like mine in the past week?"

She gives me a hard stare. "I have no idea. We turn over a lot of stock."

Luke nudges me. "Let's try the other place." He compresses the box into the crook of his arm.

I turn to him, but he's already out the door.

Trooping back outside and onto busy pavement, anxious thoughts hijack me. *What if I can't find it?* I push questions out of my mind and pin my hope on the second shop.

Dull thuds beside me. Crumpled under Luke's arm, the bottom of Shirley's box hangs open.

Luke hurls the ripped cardboard across the pavement. Books and loose photos are strewn around his feet. A gust of wind catches the photos, sending them floating towards the road. Luke scrambles to retrieve them before they're lost under car wheels and down grids. He spins around. "Marvel! Are you going to help or what?"

At my feet splays one of Shirley's journals and I pick it up. Its pages flutter in the breeze, then blow apart, revealing a pencil sketch. I clutch it to my chest. Every detail matches. *Now, I understand.*

"I should be able to get most of it in my bag." I kneel down and help Luke salvage the box's contents, stuffing the photos and journals into my backpack.

A gentle tug on my arm. "You had a vision then, didn't you? You got that faraway look." Noa's eyes fill with concern.

"Yeah, kind of." I heave my backpack over my shoulder and smile. "I'll tell you later."

The second pawn shop has a red and gold frontage with huge letters advertising twenty-four-hour loans and the best gold prices in town. Electronic doors glide open. I head straight for the glass cabinet and track every row of glinting jewellery. My heart sinks.

The shop assistant clears his throat. "Can I help you?"

Luke nudges me. "Marvel?" His eyes flick from a set of old coins to a Rolex.

I fish out the skull ring and uncurl my palm. "I'm looking for a ring that matches this one."

The man's grey hair is parted to the side and slicked down. Patches of sweat creep out from the underarms of his white shirt. He pushes up his bifocals and peers at the ring. "Hmm. Yes, it looks familiar. The owner redeemed it about ten minutes ago."

"What?" I clench the ring so tight, it gouges into my skin. "Do you have a photo?"

The man scratches his head and flakes of dandruff float onto the glass cabinet. "No. We only photograph items if they're going out for online auction."

Noa sends me a sympathetic glance.

Luke bolts out the door and runs up and down the street in a fruitless hunt for Grant. *He'll be long gone.*

"Is everything okay, Madam?" says the shop assistant, his voice rising.

"Yes." A thought pricks me. It's worth a shot. "Do you remember if the other ring had the same inscription on the inside?" I show him the maker's mark and hold my breath.

His face lights up. "Oh, yes. I do believe I made a note of that in the description." He taps into a computer and scans the screen. "Aha. Yes. Maker's inscription, M.A engraved next to hallmark." Over the top of his glasses, his watery blue eyes meet mine. "Unusual things stand out. Take care of your ring. It's beautifully made and quite valuable." He smiles.

Breath streams out. "I will. Thank you." *Value isn't always measured in money.*

Luke wanders out of the Indian takeaway carrying a grease-stained paper bag and hands out naan bread. "Right, what next? Back to Grant's house of horrors?" He swipes an imaginary softball bat through the air. "You'll need me if you want that ring back."

A chunk of soft bread gums my mouth. I manage a grunt and firm shake of my head.

Luke looks disappointed. "Oh." He screws up the bag and chucks it into a bin. "May as well get off then. Good to catch up."

A question sparks and I grab the sleeve of Luke's hoody. "Hey, when did you stop dealing?"

He turns back. "I got involved with Youth Aid around June, so stopped then. Why?"

I frown. "Nothing. Just trying to piece together a timeline."

Luke high fives Noa, then salutes me and disappears around the corner.

Swallowing down the rest of the bread, I try to connect dots in my head and figure out my next move. Groping inside my backpack, I pull out Shirley's journal and leaf through the pages until I find the sketch. "Here, look. We can't give up."

Noa stares at Shirley's drawing.

"That's what Grant looks like to me. It's identical." I trace my finger around the pencil drawing of Grant's black aura. Darker segments like tentacles splinter from its periphery. Next to it is a sketch of the skull ring and Shirley's even coloured in the ruby eyes. "Shirley is Vince's mother and she's been dead twenty years. She's been bugging me for a while." I look up. "I think she wanted me to see this."

"She was a decent artist. Really nice shading and her ring drawing is spot on." He lifts his gaze. "Do you see that black shadow around him all the time?"

A chill passes through me. "Yes. It's gross."

I crouch by a shopfront and wait for Noa to finish eating. Did Shirley come back to remind me I still have work to do? To reassure me I'm on the right track? I'm not sure. Moving a step closer to nailing Grant is like adding a new skate trick to my collection. Soon, I'll have the complete set. Today, I proved Vince's ring matches Alex's. *Stick that fact in your notebook, Edmonds.*

"Taxi's here," says Noa, moving to the kerb. "Want a lift?"

I help Noa with his crutches, then clamber inside the car. "We're changing tack. It's not the ring we need to find."

Confusion flickers across his face. "Oh. Okay."

"We need to find the jeweller. And one who accepts bitcoin."

CHAPTER NINETEEN

Dad roars up the driveway in the Honda and blasts the horn.

I jump out of the way, throwing out my hands. *Why is he so over the top?*

Sadie's in the passenger seat with her snakeskin handbag resting on her lap. She rolls her eyes at him.

The window whirs down, squeaking all the way. "How was school? You heading out?" says Dad.

"School was fine. I'm meeting Noa." Remembering a question, I blurt, "When did shops start accepting bitcoin?"

"Not sure. It was only created in 2009." His eyes narrow. "Why?"

I lower my gaze to the driveway and mumble, "It's nothing."

Dad gets out and pushes his bum against the car door to close it. "Nothing my arse. If you know anything, you must go to the police."

"And I will *if* I find something."

Dad sighs. "Hmm. Don't trust everything those spirits reveal to you." He pats my shoulder. "Alright, just be careful."

Spirits only get me so far, Dad.

Sadie walks around the car and grabs my arms. "Oh, Marvella, we just visited Vince. The difference from last time …" Tears fill her eyes. "I'm getting my grandson back."

Dad grunts. "Yeah, he's finally seen the light about Grant. Psychologist told him he's a victim of coercive control and Grant's a malignant narcissist. Christ."

"I prefer the term evil bastard, Dad."

"Ha. Nice." He locks the car and heads inside.

Sadie pulls me closer. "Are you alright?" Her worried eyes search my face.

All the stuff I haven't told her about swirls through my mind and I bite my lip hard. "I'm fine." I fake a smile. "It's great Dad went to see Vince."

"I'm always here for you. Until the day they carry me out of there in a box." She glances to her house.

I swallow. "I know."

◆

The park's full of little kids on bikes and I press my lips together. They're a hazard. The kid in front of me weaves and wobbles across the path, slowing down then speeding up every time I attempt to overtake. On the bend, I go for it and hammer the floor, sailing past him. My rumbling wheels frighten birds from trees and a flock of them soar, wings flapping into the sky.

Noa's ahead of me on his crutches.

"Hey." I jump off my board and run to catch him up.

"Hi." His smile is tight.

"How's your ankle?"

He avoids my eyes. "Yeah, seems okay. I've got another appointment next week."

I wade through long grass and follow Noa to the bench. My heart sinks lower with every step.

Noa lets his crutches fall into the grass, then meets my gaze and sighs. "We've got a problem." He flops onto the bench. "Mum talked to the priest this morning."

I tip my head back to the sky and stare at dark clouds congregating above us.

"He showed Mum Bible quotes and passages from the Catechism denouncing what you do."

Angry tears brim over. "Why did you choose my special place to tell me this?" I turn sharply to Noa.

He screws his eyes up tight. "She doesn't want me to see you, thinks you're bringing shame on our family." He meets my gaze. "I thought religion was all about bringing people together, not dividing them."

The air grows cold and I zip up my hoody. "I've had Deuteronomy quoted to me so many times, that section about being an abomination to the Lord."

My thoughts go back to the bullies at my old school, St Joseph's. Some of them were fed these quotes by their parents. I remember Sadie's words. "Sadie would disagree."

He shuffles closer. "How?"

"To commit necromancy—communicating with the dead—you have to divine spirit, call it up in some way and I've never done that." I stare ahead. "I don't want to come between you and your mum. I've seen what grudges can do." The darkening sky dulls the colour of leaves, grass and shrubs, turning them navy.

Noa exhales. "I'm not going anywhere, Marvel. Religion's like abstract art, people interpret its meaning in different ways. You're my friend and we're in this together."

A ladybird ambles up a blade of grass by my feet and its weight bends the tapered end so far it doubles over. All I do is create problems for Noa: his leg, his portfolio and now his mum. His life would be a lot easier without me in it. "If you want to bail, I totally understand."

He wraps his arm around me and smiles. "Nope. Not after I spent all morning googling jewellers."

"What?"

Noa hands me a list. "The one's crossed off don't accept bitcoin." He points to two names. "One of these is in South Island, so that just leaves this one in Auckland."

My spirits lift and I look up the Auckland jeweller

on my phone. "Some serious bling." The rings are beautifully crafted and very pricey. There's not much below a thousand bucks. "Hmm. Nothing remotely skull-like, though."

Noa leans in to look at the images on my screen. "Maybe Grant bought them off the Dark Web?"

The interior of Grant's apartment flashes up. Every item down to the colour of the walls had been carefully chosen to fit his weird gothic fantasy. "I reckon a control freak like him would want to see the rings before shelling out thousands."

A thought panics me, but I quell it and reassure myself. *Grant doesn't know I'm onto him.*

I check the shop opening times. "It's by appointment only." My eyes wander to Noa's joggers and hoody, then down to my ripped jeans and scuffed trainers. "We'll have to seriously smarten up our act. At least look like we can afford to blow a few grand on a ring."

"Easy as." He looks up at me and grins. His face falls. "What's up? You look like someone died."

"We've got *one* chance. We can't mess it up."

Noa searches my face. "What do you mean?"

"If they're as unique as he says, then Grant's bought both rings from this jeweller. If the jeweller gets suspicious, I guarantee the first person he'll contact will be—"

His eyes widen. "And the evidence disappears."

My hand whacks the bench seat. "He can't get

away with it." I tap into my phone and press submit. "Get out your best clothes." I turn to Noa. "I booked a slot for tomorrow after school."

Noa rubs his hands together. "Sweet. I'll tell Mum I'm meeting Luke."

Only a few months ago, hanging out with Luke would've been the greater sin, now it's me. Light rain falls and I plunge my hand into wet grass to retrieve Noa's crutches. "I'll think of a way to change her mind." I hand the crutches over. "You already lost your dad. I can't bear for you to lose your mum as well."

Noa looks down. "My brothers and sisters really love you. I can lie and still see you, but they can't. It's breaking their hearts."

A lump forms in my throat. I hug Noa, becoming lost in the warmth of his body and the smell of damp earth around me. My thoughts jump to little Teuila and how her big brown eyes flood me with love. There has to be something I can do. The only person who might know how to deal with a zealot like Emmeline is Sadie. It drives me crazy that at seventeen I still need my grandmother, but she really is my only hope.

I pull away and shove my wet skateboard under one arm. "I have to go. See you tomorrow."

◆

Sadie's bringing the bin in, even though Dad tells her every week to leave it for him.

She stoops and tugs it up the driveway, exposing a pale bony wrist as the sleeve of her coral-pink blouse rides up.

Running after her, I shout, "Sadie, I'll get it."

She waves me away. "No, no. I can manage." Positioning the bin behind the trellis fence, Sadie turns to me. "What's happened?"

Tears fill my eyes. "Noa's mum talked to a priest about me."

Sadie sighs. "Oh dear. You'd better come inside."

Cradling a mug of hot tea, I tuck my legs up onto the couch and drape a wool blanket over them. For the first time in ages, my thoughts settle and anxiety isn't raging through me like a herd of bulls. Since I was little, this room has never changed and I can itemise every object and piece of furniture with my eyes closed. How I wish Sadie could be locked in time, too, and never grow old. Familiar smells of furniture polish and lavender calm my soul, reassuring me this is a safe place and nothing bad happens here.

Sadie hauls out a huge tome from the bookshelf.

The words *Catholic Encyclopaedia* are embossed along the spine. She blows dust from the block of gold-leaf-edged pages and reaches to the side table for her reading glasses. Glancing up at me, she says, "You're a force for good, don't ever doubt that." Her finger runs down the page and she mumbles a number. Taking the black ribbon marker, she opens out the book and reads a passage. "The Church doesn't deny that, with a special permission of God, the souls of the departed may appear to the living, and even manifest things unknown to the latter." Sadie looks at me. "What *is* a sin, is to actively call, channel or conjure spirits. You never do."

"That's what I told Noa. How can I change Emmeline's mind?"

"Emmeline?" Sadie removes her glasses and frowns. "The same Emmeline who has five children and whose husband died a few years ago?"

"Yes. She's Noa's mum."

The book thuds shut in Sadie's hands and a plume of dust floats into the air. "Good Lord, did she speak to Father Peter about *you*?"

"I don't know the priest's name. How do you know Emmeline?"

"We're in the same parish." Sadie rams the book between a gap on the shelf. "I read palms for years at the church fair. Made thousands of dollars for the new church roof. Father Peter didn't have a problem with that, did he?" She turns and glares at me. "I dread to think what tall tales Emmeline ran to him with. Ridiculous."

"So, you think there's a chance she may change her mind?"

"Don't worry, I'll sort it out." Sadie shakes her head and stares out of the window. "What on earth was he thinking? I've talked about you so many times."

A mixture of relief and confusion whirls inside me but there's a sadness too. I'm outgrowing Sadie and opportunities for her to help me are running out fast. I almost tell her about Grant, then change tack. "I know why Shirley appeared to me."

"I knew you'd work it out," says Sadie, still staring through the window.

"She drew the skull ring in her journal." I inhale. "I think she came back to thank me for saving Vince."

Sadie's gaze shifts to me. She hesitates. "Anything else?"

Grant's aura flashes up and I shiver. "No."

Sadie's blue eyes don't leave mine. "Be careful, Marvella. We both know Shirley didn't wait twenty years just to say thank you."

My short cut across Sadie's garden backfires. Box hedge scratches my bare legs and a fence paling jabs my thigh. Serves me right for not telling her the truth. I stand by my decision, though. What can she do to help? Convincing Emmeline I'm not a devil worshipper is enough of a challenge for her. I unlock my front door and remember the drawings in the journal. Shirley wants me to nail Grant and I'm determined not to let that slippery snake of a man get away with his crimes.

I open my wardrobe door and unhook the few garments worthy of a coat hanger. A simple denim shift dress will have to do. It doesn't scream money, but then neither does Grant. How he could afford to drop a few grand on a ring, when he was months away from financial ruin, never added up. I know what the weak link is and I'll get the evidence to prove it. A bolt of fear shoots through me, reminding me what Grant is capable of. I push it from my mind. Spirits led me this far, now it's up to me.

CHAPTER TWENTY

I recheck the street address on my phone, then search shop fronts for numbers. "It has to be around here." Time's running out and my heart cranks up another level, sending hot panic through me.

An older woman in stilettos and garish make-up struts towards me, muttering under her breath. "Excuse me," she says, indignant.

I stop zigzagging and move aside to let her pass. Dusting down my cheap chain store dress, I tell myself to chill.

Noa squints down a narrow alleyway between a fancy art shop and one selling designer homeware. "Is that it?"

An engraved bronze plate on the wall identifies the shop. I silently curse it for being so well hidden and making us ten minutes late.

Noa's breath steams a patch onto the shop's metal door. The top buttons of his fitted black shirt are undone, drawing my gaze to a V-shape of bare brown chest.

A voice crackles through the intercom. "Yes? Do you have an appointment?"

"Hello, err, it's Julia Fleming." *Why am I so crap at lying?* I take a deep breath. "Sorry I'm late. I couldn't find the shop."

A sigh filters through the intercom. Silence, then deep within the shop a bolt shunts and a key turns. The same sounds repeat, growing louder.

I glance across to Noa, who raises his eyes and tucks in his shirt.

A jangle of keys and one last turn, then the metal door swings back

A gangly man appears in a navy suit, glasses hanging on a cord around his neck. "Hello, Miss Fleming." He speaks with a posh English accent. His eyes shift to Noa. "Hello, Sir. Watch the step."

He waves us inside and through another door, then draws apart bottle-green velvet curtains to reveal a dark circular room that smells of old wood. Illuminated glass cabinets glow in a semi-circle around us.

Unease grows and my confidence plummets. Heart pounding, I fight the urge to leg it and try to focus on what I have to do.

"It's like a museum," whispers Noa.

His soft voice is calming and my tension loosens its grip.

Behind me, the jeweller's heavy breathing disturbs the hairs on my neck. Keys rattle and a lock clunks into place, then dense silence descends, like being wrapped in layers of cotton wool. Brisk movement disturbs air to my left and a switch clicks. The room floods with light, radiating from a glittering chandelier suspended from the vaulted ceiling. The jeweller stands like a sentry behind the cabinets and tilts up his chin. Light reflects off his bare scalp and his lean, hollow-cheeked face is expressionless. "What can I do for you?" He plucks an orange handkerchief from his top pocket and cleans his glasses.

"Err." I close my eyes and imagine the room is a skate park and I'm dangling over the edge of the half-pipe, about to drop in. *I can do it.* "I'm looking for a ring for my eighteenth birthday. Something kind of—" Dad pops into my head. "Something punk rock." I cringe.

The man straightens out his handkerchief and performs a sequence of folds like origami, then replaces it in his pocket. He slides his glasses along his nose and peers over the black metal frames, fixing me in a watery gaze. "We're not in the business of edgy or trendy or—God forbid ..." he lets out a long sigh, "punk rock." He accentuates every syllable. "As you can see from the display, we craft classic cut gemstone rings and wedding bands." His long fingers travel along the glass cabinet, catching a loose sheet of paper which becomes airborne and glides to my feet.

I hand it back, noticing the courier stamp in one corner and a name in copperplate print. The name reminds me of one of Dad's dumb T-shirts.

"Thank you." He purses his lips. "Do any of these interest you?"

I scan the jewellery display. It's a feast of sparkling colour and precious metal, nothing skull-like at all. *Think, Marvel.*

I look up. "I've a substantial budget."

The man straightens. "I see."

Noa nudges me and writes in the air with a finger. *Of course.*

I point to a gold and ruby cluster ring, knowing I wouldn't be seen dead in it. "Could I have a look at this one?"

The jeweller reaches under the counter and grasps the ring in a cloth, then passes it to me.

I examine the heavy gold and find the hallmark. There's no other inscription and my heart sinks. I slide it onto my finger and I'm a kid again, raiding Sadie's jewellery box and parading around in her high-heeled shoes.

Noa coughs and I follow his gaze to a glass cabinet on the far right, where a tray of rings is missing from one of the rows.

"That's a tray of wedding rings." The jeweller falters. "It's out the back for polishing." He leers at me. "Something to consider for the future, maybe?"

Heat rushes into my cheeks and I scramble to change the subject. "Do you make speciality rings to order?" I hand the cluster ring back to him, but he avoids my eyes.

"Occasionally," he mutters. "Can you be more specific about what you actually want?" His voice hardens. "I've another appointment shortly."

Frantic thoughts race through my mind. There's no other option. "I want a skull ring."

The jeweller winces. "No, dear. This really isn't the right establishment for you."

Hope drains away. *Why did I ever think I could pull this off?*

The man strides around us with his nose in the air, mumbling under his breath. A metallic jangle rings out as he yanks apart the curtains. He props open the door for us to leave. "Sorry I can't be of more help, Miss Marvel." He forces a smile. "Maybe try the mall."

Miss Marvel? Shit.

I crouch by a wall and thump my temples. "We're too late. We need that missing tray. Damn Grant."

Noa's voice is weak. "I might have to sit down."

I spring up and grab his arm. "There's a cafe over the road. Let's go."

A sheen of sweat coats Noa's brow and his face turns a sickly shade of brown. Raging thoughts mix with guilt and underneath them, a growing well of fear rises up.

Stepping into the road, I stop traffic with my palm and help Noa across.

The cafe is busy. A waitress sets down a tray of freshly baked scones on the counter. Their sweet cinnamon smell reminds me of Sadie's apple pie. Background chatter clouds my thinking and there's a heaviness in the pit of my stomach knowing Grant's one step ahead of me. I order two Cokes at the counter. Thoughts of what to do next stream through my mind, until one stops and embeds itself, teasing me with its sheer craziness. It's probably breaking the law, too, but what choice do I have? *Fuck it.* I pull out my phone and search up the jeweller's website. Choosing the Book Appointment header from the drop-down box, I type Luke's name, then press submit.

Noa sinks into a chair and passes me his crutches. "That's better. Standing for too long makes it ache." He wipes his forehead with the back of his hand.

I move closer, scraping my chair across concrete floor. "How soon can Luke get here?"

His eyes widen. "Luke? Why?"

"Just trust me."

"If he can borrow his brother's motorbike, then maybe twenty minutes."

"Ask him to meet us here. I snared him the last appointment slot at the jewellers." I take a sip of Coke and crunch down hard on a piece of ice, giving myself brain freeze.

Noa gives me a hard stare. "Okay. Then, you'll tell me what's going on?"

"Yep." My gaze shifts to the street, travelling up and down the rows. "There's one. Back in a minute."

I race across the road, weaving through parked cars

and slow-moving traffic to the opposite pavement. Dodging an elderly couple and a Shih Tzu with a pink satin bow on its head, I burst through automatic doors and come to an abrupt stop at the queue inside the post office. *Great.* Beside a fat woman in a floral pantsuit is a rack of courier bags. I choose the smallest one with the most secure tracking.

Back at the cafe, I stuff crumpled napkins and sugar sachets into the bag until it feels reasonably full, then write the address of the jewellery shop on the label. I push doubt from my mind, because if I think about this too hard, I'll totally lose my nerve.

"Luke's on his way." Noa frowns. "What are you doing?"

"Promise you won't try and dissuade me?" I reach for his hands.

Concern fills his eyes. "Marvel, you're trembling."

Before I change my mind, I whisper my plan to Noa. "Do you think you can do it?"

Noa nods.

"I'll phone Edmonds as soon as we have proof."

A motorbike pulls up outside the cafe and the driver takes off his helmet.

I drain my Coke. "He's here." The cold liquid trickles down my throat and I shiver. "Sure you feel up to it?"

Noa grabs the courier parcel and shoves it under his arm. "Let's go."

Luke's hair sticks to his temples. He loops his arm through the helmet and shakes his head. "Things I do for you, cuz. I hooned it down that motorway."

I step forward. "Thanks Luke. It was all my idea." I gush out my plan without even pausing for breath, and wait for Luke to tell me I'm completely mental.

"Any security guards inside?" says Luke, his eyes flicking over shopfronts.

I exhale. "Err. No." I zip open my backpack and rummage around until I find the ring, then hand it to him. "Memorise this inscription."

Luke's gaze lifts to mine. "Got it."

"We'll walk with you. Come on." My eyes land across the road, on the narrow alleyway leading to the jewellers and my stomach tightens. I look at Luke. "No violence."

Luke's already at the kerb. "Yeah, yeah. Don't worry."

I wait until Luke prods the jeweller's intercom, then hide around the corner with Noa and take slow deep breaths. This is our last chance. We blow this and Grant gets away with it.

A text pings and Noa jumps. "It's Luke. I'm up."

Staying close to Noa, I scan above the jeweller's door for cameras. There's nothing obvious.

He presses the buzzer. "Auckland Couriers."

The jeweller's irritable voice. "You already delivered today. What's going on?"

Noa shoots me a panicked glance, then turns back

to the intercom. "I don't know. You're on my list, sir. I need a signature."

The intercom crackles.

Noa's tone hardens. "I can't wait. I'm parked on yellow lines."

"Alright, alright. I'm coming."

Locks shift from inside the shop and I nudge Noa. "Drop it."

He props the parcel against the door and follows me back around the corner, his breath catching with every step.

My heart pounds so fast it's making me light-headed and I squat by some stinking bins. It's down to Luke now. I imagine the crack of a baseball bat against the jeweller's head and a wave of nausea rolls through me.

Noa taps my shoulder. "We should get back to the cafe." He propels forwards and grimaces.

Oh God, was Noa lying just to help me out?

Inside the cafe, I take sip after sip of water until my glass is empty, then pour myself another, as various doom-laden scenarios power through my mind. What if the jeweller catches Luke rummaging around for the missing tray of rings and calls the cops? Or what if Luke veers off-plan and gets caught stealing the matching ring instead of photographing it? Putting my trust in a loose cannon like Luke is shredding my nerves and if he fucks up, then Grant remains a free man.

Noa drums his fingers on the table and glances nervously out of the window.

I'm halfway through my third glass of water when a dark blur catches my eye and a chair scrapes the floor.

"That was cutting it fine. No way was he gone for two minutes. The old fella was fast as with those locks." Luke dumps his helmet on an empty chair and downs a glass of water.

I grip the edge of the table.

A smile grows across Luke's face. He pulls out his phone and skims it across the table towards me.

The photo of the ring is a bit blurry, but good enough. The M.A. inscription is indisputable. *We did it.* "Thanks, Luke."

Luke jolts forward. "Yeah, lucky I checked underneath the counter for that missing tray. It was sat there under a cloth. Just as well, because I wouldn't have had enough time to search the back. He'd have caught me red-handed."

My guts lurch. Time is running out. No doubt the fake parcel will trigger a CCTV check. I grab Luke's phone and send myself the photo, then text it to Edmonds with the caption: *cold, hard fact.*

Edmonds' caller ID lights up my phone.

I explain about the skull rings. "The inscriptions match."

Any second I expect him to lose it, tell me I'm a meddling fool and hang up, but instead there's silence down the line.

I go for it. "Grant bought the ring for Vince's birthday in June and he paid for it with bitcoin." It's a huge assumption, and if he asks me to prove it I'm screwed. I take a quick breath. "The same bitcoin address as—

Edmonds' voice is gruff. "I understand." Eventually, he says I could be onto something.

The phone's slippery in my sweaty hand. "You need to hurry. Grant tipped off the jeweller." I hang up. But instead of victory, the only sensation I feel is fear. The web is closing in and I dread what ends Grant will resort to, to avoid getting caught. The skull ring digs into the top of my thigh and I reach into my pocket and pull it out. Without thinking, words spurt, "Sometimes, you have to delve into shadow to bring out the light."

Outside the cafe, Luke sits astride his motorbike and adjusts his helmet.

Noa pinches my arm.

"Ouch. What the hell?" I turn sharply to Noa, but he's staring ahead.

The jeweller stands in front of us with his hands on his hips and a face like thunderous sky.

"I don't know what you three are up to, but I *will* find out." A bead of white spit forms at the corner of his mouth. He wipes it away with his orange handkerchief, then storms off, scrunching the orange fabric in his hand.

Noa yelps and his face contorts with pain.

It's all my fault. Pushing him to the limit with my stupid plan. All the stress has broken him. "Oh my God, I'm so sorry." There are a few chairs outside the cafe and I reach for one, dragging it towards Noa. "Here, sit down."

His eyes fill with worry. "The jeweller?"

I swallow. "It's okay, the police are—"

"Cuz, you want to get that ankle looked at. Its probably cracked again where the bone's weak." Luke jumps off his bike and holds out his hand. "Get on. I'll take you to the hospital." He helps Noa onto the bike and passes him a spare helmet.

My phone rings. It's Dad, asking me if I'm home. Worry tinges his voice.

A chill shoots through me. "No. Why?"

He's at the supermarket with Mum and forgot Sadie's shopping list. She's not answering her mobile or landline.

Noa's eyes meet mine. "Be careful. Promise me."

I nod, but already the street is closing in, engulfing me in sickening panic.

Luke revs the bike and roars off down the street.

Alone in the middle of a strange suburb, my thoughts scramble, leaving me frozen to the pavement. Desperately trying to remember the way home or which bus to catch, I manage a few seconds of focus before panic takes over. Stuck at a red light is an empty taxi and I run down the street towards it. I open the passenger door and yell at the driver, "Taylor's Hill as fast as you can. It's an emergency."

The driver glances across. His gaze wanders over my face and down to my white-knuckled hands. "Okay. But please put your seatbelt on."

Cursing Auckland's snarled traffic, I will every traffic light to turn green. Halfway home, Dad texts to say he's on his way.

The taxi pulls in to the kerb and slows. Wheels still turning, my clammy hand depresses the door lever and I chuck a twenty at the driver, then stumble in the direction of Sadie's house.

Scrabbling under the terracotta pot for the spare key, my fingers so shaky I almost drop the key between the decking. I fumble with the lock, but something's not right and when I try the handle the door's already unlocked. It swings open and my eyes latch onto the stopped clock hanging on the wall, then the smashed lamp in the middle of the hallway floor. It's cold and draughty, like a window's been left open. I kick aside the lamp and run down the hallway, glancing sideways into Sadie's bedroom where clothes and broken objects litter the floor. Acidic bile forms in the back of my throat. I crash through the lounge door and vomit over fragments of glass.

"Sadie!"

Blood leeches from a head wound, dripping down her face and onto the chair arm.

She groans and mumbles something, but I can't understand her.

My voice trembles. "It's okay, Sadie. Hang on." I grab a clump of tissues from the box on the side-table and press the wound. The tissues sink into Sadie's scalp and I retch. With one hand I phone an ambulance, then Edmonds, and then Dad.

"Marvel, what is it?" says Dad.

Speech won't come. Tears roll down my face and I kneel onto broken glass, staring at the shattered lounge window. A familiar smell catches and my world crumbles. The smell of woody aftershave is a dagger straight into my heart.

"Marvel! For Christ's sake, talk to me," shouts Dad.

"He hurt Sadie."

CHAPTER TWENTY-ONE

Mum prises my hand from Sadie's. "They need to take her now. Dad's going in the ambulance."

I kiss Sadie's forehead and my lips brush against bandages wrapped around her head, already stained with her blood.

Squeezing Sadie's hand again, I whisper, "We'll get him." Her hand is cool and I tuck it under the blanket covering her.

"Right, let's go," says one of the paramedics.

I stand back while they manoeuvre the stretcher across the lounge and down the hallway, glass crunching under its wheels.

Dad's alongside the paramedics, firing questions at them, but they don't know the answers. His face is pale and there's blood on his favourite Misfits T-shirt. He looks at me. "She's going to be alright."

His words fall flat, like he's trying to convince me skating in the rain won't wreck my board.

Mum pulls me over to the couch and drapes a

blanket over my legs. She places a mug of tea on the side table.

The sour smell of vomit taints the air and I tug the blanket up to cover my nose. The tea is sweet. Noises carry from the hallway and Edmonds appears at the doorway, eyes wandering around the room, then landing on me.

"Forensics are coming in. Your mother's studio looks intact, but I'd advise you not to touch anything until they've finished."

I slop tea over the blanket. "What do you mean?"

"Your house was ransacked, too. Burglar got in through your bedroom window."

Anger bubbles up inside me. *He was looking for the ring.* "It was Grant. I smelt his aftershave."

Edmonds sighs.

I could tell him about bad energy stopping the clock, Shirley's picture, Grant's aura, but I'd be wasting my breath. He'll get his *cold, hard facts* eventually, but by then it'll be too late.

Mum runs in. "Sadie's jewellery's gone." She clutches her head.

Edmonds frowns. "I understand how upsetting this is, but you're contaminating the scene. Both of you need to wait in the art studio."

◆

Grey light sucks colour from Mum's studio. Her paintings surround me, their swirls and waves transformed into ghostly shadows. The two-seater couch is snug and I'm submerged under a mountain of blankets and quilts. A cold cup of tea sits on the floor next to me. I must have slept for hours.

My phone beeps. It's a message from Dad. Sadie needed ten stitches in her scalp, but there's no fracture or bleed on her brain. They're monitoring her overnight. She's had a cup of tea and a sandwich.

My hand shakes and relief cascades through me. I scroll through my messages. Nothing from Noa, so I text him, asking if he's okay.

Muffled voices outside the door.

Edmonds comes in. "You alright?" There's dark circles under his eyes.

I nod.

He sits on Mum's painting stool. "Everyone's leaving now. Forensics have finished. Your mum's cleaning up. She's ordered takeaways."

"Dad says Sadie's going to be okay." As the words leave me, it's like my brain changes gear and a different emotion kicks in. My fingernails claw at the couch fabric, wishing it was the skin of Grant's back.

"Your grandmother didn't see her assailant. He must have attacked her from behind." Edmonds clears his throat. "And I'm getting a warrant to search the jeweller's. Should be through soon."

I sit up and throw off the covers. "You need to get there *fast*."

His eyes narrow. "Why?"

"After I phoned you, the jeweller saw us with Luke. Noa distracted him with a fake courier parcel to buy Luke time to find a matching ring. The jeweller will have seen the CCTV and told Grant."

Alex's skull ring juts out of my jeans pocket. "I won't be needing this anymore." I pause. "Sorry I didn't give it to you earlier." I pass Edmonds the ring and show him the inscription. "Cold, hard fact?"

Edmonds gives a weak smile. "There's no need to be sarcastic. Process has to be followed or else no one gets justice." He excuses himself and leaves the room to answer a call.

I think I'm allowed a little sarcasm. I've put my family in harm's way doing Edmond's job and now I have to wait for him to get his shit together. Frustrating doesn't even cut it. Every second he's faffing around with process is a second he could be out there looking for Grant. If I knew where to find Grant I'd be there in a heartbeat. *What have I got to lose?* He left Sadie for dead. I don't give a crap about law or process now.

Edmonds returns and he's ashen. He stares at the floor, then takes a deep breath and looks up. "The jeweller's dead. Strangled. CCTV smashed. His computer stolen and there's a tray of rings unaccounted for." He sighs. "The jeweller activated the panic button, but it was too late."

My blood runs cold.

Edmonds studies my face. "Marvel, is there

anything you're not telling me?" He screws up his eyes like he's in pain. "Any visions?"

"Grant's behind it. He masterminded Vince's kidnapping and now he's destroying evidence. I found the weak link and he knows it." Anger surges and my voice hardens. "I don't have proof. You *have* to trust me."

Edmonds studies my face and deliberates. "Okay. Let's hope the jeweller's records are backed up to the Cloud." He issues orders over the phone, then turns to me. "Officers are looking for Grant. A manned police vehicle will be stationed outside your house." He turns to go, then glances back. "Promise me you won't leave the house. It's too dangerous for you and your parents."

I fold my arms across my chest.

He raises his voice. "Marvel?"

"Yes. I promise." The words float off my tongue and not even a ripple of guilt troubles my conscience.

After Edmonds leaves, I stare at Mum's paintings until darkness descends and everything in the room becomes amorphous. Into the black silence, I whisper, "Let me finish this. I can do it."

A text pings. It's Noa: *Home now. Ankle okay. Just have to rest. You alright?*

I stare at my phone, debating whether to put a downer on his good news, and remember I promised to tell him everything. The text box turns green. Think I overdid it a bit with the angry face emojis, but too late now.

OMG. Should I come over? Luke's crashing here. He can bring me.

I text back that I'm fine and getting an early night.

Don't go anywhere without us.

Flicking him a thumbs up emoji, I add a heart emoji, then delete it.

An early night is the last thing I intend on getting. How can I sleep after what's happened? Figuring out Grant's next move means getting inside the head of a malignant narcissist. Whatever that is. Sitting on the end of my bed, a draught from my boarded-up window ripples the curtains, blowing cool night air against my face. Scrolling through articles about narcissism, I whisper sections of text, "Grandiose self-importance, no empathy, sadism, paranoia, lack of remorse, self-destructive behaviour. Similar traits to a psychopath." One phrase hits me hard: *Seeks to win at all costs.*

How can Grant win? The jeweller's dead and he stole the computer, which may or may not be backed up. If it is, he's lost. *So, what will he do next?* The click of the front door closing disturbs my thoughts. Footsteps carry from the kitchen, then water thunders into the kettle. Dad's home from the hospital.

Desperate to pee, I sneak to the bathroom, trying not to bang any doors in the process. The last thing I need is an interrogation from Dad. On the bathroom floor by the overflowing laundry hamper lies Dad's bloodstained

Misfits T-shirt. The sight of it triggers a memory of the paper sheet floating to my feet at the jewellers and the company name beneath the courier logo. What did it say exactly? Misfit, then another word that sounded like artist. M.A. *The inscription!* The name's on the tip of my tongue. Got it. *Misfit Artisan.* The maker of the skull rings. *Shit.* Goosebumps pop along my arms and a chilling thought strikes me. There're two possibilities: Grant knows he's losing, switches to self-destruct mode and takes everyone down with him, or, intent on winning, he continues destroying evidence, which means his next target will be the ring maker's records. Either way, the maker's life's in danger. And so is mine.

A mug clunks against the kitchen bench and the toaster rack clicks down. I wish the kitchen wasn't so close to my bedroom. Heart thumping, I type *Misfit Artisan* into my phone and to my relief, it's not far, maybe fifteen minutes if I skate there. No way am I involving Dad in this, so the only way out is through my boarded-up window. And if I don't move fast, the maker's going to die.

A thick sheet of plywood's nailed to the window frame. I push against it with all my weight, but it doesn't budge. All this effort to keep me safe from Grant, and now I'm breaking free to reach *him*. I creep into the hallway and place my ear against the lounge door, listening for any sign of Dad. Has he taken his tea and toast to bed? Crashed out in the armchair? A snore carries to me and I depress the door handle.

A piece of half-eaten toast hangs from Dad's fingers and a milk skin's formed on the surface of his tea. *Yuck.* Tiptoeing past him, a loud snore startles me and I freeze. A horrible thought sparks. Could this be the last time I ever see him? Dad would do anything to protect me. Imagine the pain of losing him. That would be the same pain he'd feel if I died. And the same goes for Mum, too. I can't be a lamb for slaughter. A skateboard is no use against someone as callous as Grant. *Remember, he wants to win at all costs.*

In the hallway, I text Noa the maker's address, adding the words, *Ring maker. This is Grant's next move.* Then, I send another message: *Stay home. Send Luke. With every weapon he's got.*

Outside, I crouch behind Dad's Honda. A police car's stationed at the end of the driveway and there's two officers inside. A few metres of driveway separates me from the shadow of Sadie's backyard. It's a risk I have to take. I crane my neck around the wheel of the Honda. The two cops are chatting. Now's my chance. I bolt across the patch of exposed driveway and over Sadie's picket fence, landing in a prickly shrub. Screwing up my face in pain, I drag myself out and resist the urge to yell as thorns tear at my skin and clothes. Messages ping on my phone and I turn it to silent, knowing Noa will be trying to talk me out of it or persuading me to tell Edmonds. But Edmonds wants proof, not speculation. And even though he's warming to the truth about my visions, no spirit has forced my hand this time. This is all on me.

The far side of Sadie's house never gets much sun and the concrete pavers are slimy and slippery with moss. Various garden tools stack against the house, glinting under rays of moonlight. Paranoid about setting off next door's dog, I force myself to move slowly, against the surging tide of adrenaline pulsing through my body. Musty smells of damp earth and rotting vegetation surround me. My feet squelch across Sadie's front lawn and I tug my back foot out of the soggy ground and onto pavement.

Skateboard wheels rumble beneath me and cold air whips my face. Energy burns and my anxiety transforms into forward momentum at a blistering pace. I anticipate every pothole, sharp bend and corner. No hazard fazes me. Every so often, I check behind for a police car, but the road's clear.

I find the street number for *Misfit Artisan*. The 1970s brick and tile house is at the end of a long driveway and high hedging borders both sides. No lights are on. I send a text: *Here.* My anxiety has nowhere to go now and it rises up, making my hands tremble and my heart pound. I hide behind a block wall and try to stop my teeth chattering. Faint engine noise grows louder and I peer around the wall.

Luke's here. And Noa. *What the hell?*

I march over. "The hospital told you to rest. Grant's a psycho, he'll pick you off. You're easy prey."

Noa climbs off the back of the motorbike and sets down his crutches. "Safety in numbers. Do you honestly think I'd let you do this without me?" His eyes glint under streetlight.

My face goes hot and I stare at the ground.

"Right. Zip it you two. Follow me." Luke ducks down by the hedge and unfastens his backpack. "What do you want? Knife, baseball bat or pepper spray?"

Oh God. "Err, I have my skateboard."

Luke sighs. "Grant's just taken out the jeweller. You'll need more than that. Here." He thrusts a can of pepper spray into my hand. "Stick it in your back pocket." Luke pulls out the baseball bat and passes Noa a small kitchen knife. "You can have this."

Noa weighs the knife in his hand. "If he's here, we get out and phone the cops."

"We can't let him kill another innocent person. Remember how long the cops took to arrive with Vince?"

"She's right. We need to take him out," says Luke.

"What if he has a gun?" Noa's words hang in the air.

I glance at Luke. He's staring down the driveway and thumping the baseball bat against his palm. "Can you smell smoke?"

A narrow plume of smoke rises into the sky from behind the maker's house. "Who lights a fire at two in the morning?" I say.

"Come on." Luke crouches by the hedge and runs

down the driveway, signalling for us to follow him around the side of the house.

Smoke catches in my throat as I run and I stifle a cough. The air is hazy and there's a distant crackle of fire. Unease creeps over me and fear chips away my courage. I wait for Noa to catch up, then whisper, "I've got a really bad feeling about this. I'm texting Edmonds."

Noa leans against rough brick. "I already did."

Luke beckons to me.

Steeling myself, I crawl underneath the window and stay close behind Luke. Dim light glows from the furthest window. I shiver and sickening dread comes over me. Catching my breath, I mutter, "He's here."

Luke peeks over the window ledge, then drops down. "Fuck." He pulls his hoody sleeve down over his hand, reaches up and punches the end of the baseball bat through the glass. He undoes the latch and the window swings open. "He's on the patio burning piles of paper. A woman's tied up in there." He tilts his head to the open window.

Petrol fumes drift from inside and my gaze shifts to the window. "I can do it."

Luke cranes around me. "Cuz, you're back up. I'm going after the weirdo."

I kneel and steal a glance through the window. A woman's bound to a chair and next to her, papers litter the floor by an open filing cabinet. Her hair and clothes are soaking wet. In front of the woman is a ranchslider leading to a patio where Grant's dumping paper and a laptop into a blazing oil drum. *He's burning evidence.*

"Noa, can I swap pepper spray for your knife? She's zip tied." *And I bet it was Grant who instructed Alex to use the same ties on Vince.*

He hands me the knife. "Be careful. Cops will be here any minute."

Luke squats by the corner of the house. He turns to me and whispers sharply, "His back's turned. Go, Marvel."

I scramble over the window ledge and my feet crunch against broken glass. Leaving my skateboard by the window, I crawl over to the woman and breathe in petrol fumes. Even though Grant's on the other side of a glass door, his aura chills my bones. Crouching behind the woman, a bolt of fear shoots through me. The petrol smell stems from her.

I retrieve the knife from my back pocket and whisper, "Don't move. I'll untie you." The knife slips in my sweaty palm and my hand shakes. *Winning at all costs?* I shudder; I never imagined this would involve burning someone alive.

She mumbles into the tape sealing her mouth shut and stinking petrol drips from her hair onto the concrete floor.

Fumbling for an edge to grip, I rip the tape off her mouth.

"Ouch."

I whisper, "Sorry. Are you Misfit Artisan? I'm Marvel."

"That's my business. My name's Alison. Hurry, please."

I see-saw the knife blade through the zip tie around her ankle. It's tight against the chair leg and I push hard against the tip of the knife as I move it up and down. It snaps and scuttles across the floor. One down. Dizzy from petrol fumes, I manage to free Alison's other leg.

She jolts the plastic chair and pushes it backwards with her feet, scraping the floor and narrowly avoiding my fingers.

I pinch her arm. "Calm down, Alison."

A swishing sound as the ranchslider opens, then footsteps and an object crashes onto the floor. I peer around Alison and gasp. Shadows of grey and black flicker in the periphery of my field of vision and Luke's baseball bat rolls across polished concrete.

"Drop the knife, sweetheart."

I stand up and stagger sideways, lunging for the back of the chair. My hands slide against the wet plastic until my grip holds and I breathe, waiting for the giddiness to pass.

Luke stumbles forward, looking more pissed off than scared.

My knife clatters to the floor. I straighten up and walk in front of Alison. *If you want to burn her alive, you'll have to kill me first.*

Grant prods Luke in the back, then lifts his arm and points the gun at me.

"Still trying to hide your tracks, Grant?" I pull my shoulders back and stare into the barrel of the gun. "Pretty dumb buying Vince's ring with bitcoin, then using the same account for his ransom?"

Grant's outstretched arm shakes. "Nothing links to me."

Where are the cops? Just keep him talking. "Police are searching the jeweller's records as we speak."

Grant leers. "Do I look worried, sweetheart? Some people are so old school, they don't get round to signing up to the Cloud." The shadows around him grow, blurring his features and transforming his face into an indistinct, blotchy mess. He's self-destructing. His own aura's destroying him.

Out of the corner of my eye, Luke's foot inches towards the baseball bat.

Sadie's words come back to me: *Have faith in yourself, Marvella.* I step closer, bringing my body centimetres from the gun aimed at my heart. "I'm a psychic. Spirits led me to Vince, then pointed me in your direction. I know *all* your secrets." I take a deep breath, swallowing down bitter memory. "How dare you hurt my grandmother."

Grant tilts his head in mock sympathy. "She's still alive? That's a shame."

Hot anger flares. "You didn't have the guts to kill her." I press my chest against the gun. "Or me."

A crash from outside and flames shoot across the patio.

Grant turns around and fires the gun, shattering the glass ranchslider.

In a flash, Luke grabs the baseball bat and brings it down hard on Grant's head. "You fucking freak." He races outside. "Noa!"

My heart hits the floor. I charge outside, slipping on petrol, then jumping over glowing embers strewn across the patio. One of Noa's crutches butts up against the bottom of the oil drum, filling the air with the smell of burning rubber. I stop. An orb of white light approaches from the darkness beyond the patio. The same white light I saw the day we met. "Noa?"

Noa steps out of the darkness, leaning heavily against Luke. The smile on his face takes my breath away.

I throw my arms around them.

Luke chokes on his words. "I thought that psycho had shot you." He wipes a hand over his eyes. "Never thought I'd be so relieved to see your ugly face, cuz." He turns to me. "You okay?"

I nod, unable to speak.

Noa touches my hand. "Sorry to give you a fright. I had to lie down to knock the oil drum over. The bullet whizzed over my head."

Moans carry from the lounge and Alison yells, "Can someone untie my arms? He's waking up."

I run inside and cut open the remaining zip ties, freeing her. "Sorry. I thought he'd shot my friend."

"Thanks. Police are here."

I follow her gaze to the window as police, firefighters and paramedics file past. Revolving light reflects off their fluoro jackets. Edmonds spots me and shakes his head.

A firefighter douses the fire with a hose, leaving the patio littered with ash, soggy paper and broken bits of metal.

Officers swoop into the lounge and surround Grant while paramedics tend to him and check on Alison.

Edmonds sidles over. "Why am I always the last to know?" He sighs. "You could have all been killed."

"I acted on a hunch. I didn't have any—"

"You didn't need proof, Marvel. You had my trust."

There's disappointment in his eyes and I fight back tears. "I'm sorry."

"Excuse me. I need to give you this." Alison thrusts a piece of paper into Edmond's hand. "Donald advised me to hide a copy of Grant Dickson's order for the skull ring."

"Donald, the jeweller?" asks Edmonds. "When did he warn you?"

"Late afternoon today. I tried phoning him back around five, but it went to voicemail."

Edmonds and I exchange a look.

"Thank you. I'll need a full statement once you're feeling up to it."

A paramedic drapes a silver sheet around Alison's shoulders and ushers her away.

Edmonds scans the piece of paper and smiles. "You were right." He tilts the paper so I can read it.

My fists tighten. It's all here. Grant's personal details, the request for a skull ring and next to the method of payment is a string of letters and numbers identifying his bitcoin address.

Luke slaps Edmonds on the back. "We have to stop meeting like this, Detective. You should seriously think about hiring us as your crack team." He twitches. "I'd have bashed him sooner, but he pulled the gun on me too quick."

Edmonds rolls his eyes. "Hmm. You were all very fortunate. Safer to leave this to the professionals, don't you think?"

Luke shrugs, then turns to watch the paramedics stretcher Grant towards the waiting ambulance. His face falls. "If that psycho had shot Noa, I'd have totally finished him off."

Edmonds puts a hand on Luke's shoulder. "Take my advice. Work hard and stay out of trouble."

I retrieve Noa's damaged crutch from the wet patio and walk over to where he's sitting. I pass him the crutch. "All the rubber's melted away from the end."

"Doesn't matter. I don't need them for much longer." His gaze fixes on a set of paintings hanging on the wall. "Her taste in art matches her taste in rings."

I flick my eyes to the wall and study the three pictures. The middle one is gross, depicting men being tortured in Hell with Christ surrounded by angels, Mary and the Apostles overhead. "Who would want to look at that?"

"*The Last Judgment*, by Bosch." He looks at me. "Full on but suits the moment, I guess."

Not wanting to dwell on weird images of Heaven and Hell, I change the subject. "How's your ankle?"

"Bit sore. How are you?"

I exhale. "I'm good."

Edmonds comes over. His brow furrows. "Can I talk to you for a minute?"

I step to the side, thinking he's after another long boring statement about what happened, like the one I had to do after we found Vince.

"Someone's leaked details about you to the press." He clears his throat. "They know your psychic visions led you to Vince. No doubt the same person will pass on information about tonight."

I look into Edmond's worried eyes and at the deep lines etched into his face. "We just caught a murderer. Our lives were threatened. My grandmother was left for dead." I smile. "I think I can handle a few nosy journos."

CHAPTER TWENTY-TWO

Voices wake me up. A blast of cool air billows out my curtains, revealing two guys in overalls slotting a piece of glass into my window frame. Sounds dull from outside and, judging by the intensity of light in my bedroom, I reckon it must be around mid-morning. I roll onto my side and reach for my phone to confirm the time, but the battery's dead. After all the drama of last night, I was too exhausted to plug it in.

I stumble into the lounge where Sadie's sitting on the couch cradling a mug of tea. "Oh. You're home." Deep purple bruising extends from her forehead around to her left cheek. They've cut off her hair, revealing a line of stitches curving around her scalp. A lump forms in my throat. "How are you?"

"Don't I look a sight? It's only bruising though, it'll fade." She taps her head. "No serious damage. I was very lucky. The staff were tremendous."

I sit next to her. "I'm sorry. I never expected he would hurt you."

Sadie puts her mug down and pats my hand. "None of this was your fault." She examines my palm, tracing her finger along the lines. "You have a fully formed Line of Intuition. I saw it when you were a baby. It's the mark of true psychic ability. Shirley had it too." She locks her eyes onto mine. "It's not been easy watching you handle all this yourself, but you had to learn to accept your Gift." Her voice shakes. "I'm so proud of you."

I hesitate. "You *knew* about Grant?"

"I looked through Shirley's journal many times after she died. When you started seeing the skull ring, I remembered her drawing." She pauses and takes a deep breath. "The worst part was when you described Grant's aura and it matched Shirley's sketch."

I grasp her hands and hold back tears. "You don't need to worry about me anymore."

Sadie shakes her head. "It's a grandmother's duty to worry, Marvella." She looks away like she's deliberating whether to mention something.

"What is it?"

Sadie sighs. "Vince's palm is a different matter. Poor Shirley saw it too and it worried her sick." She turns to me. "He has a break in his Life Line which indicates trouble of great magnitude." She frowns. "And as I recall, his Life Line restarts deeper and stronger." She smiles. "You never gave up on him. Your actions carried him across that break."

Poor Sadie's been living with all this for years. What a burden to carry. "It's over now, Sadie."

"Now you understand why I don't read palms anymore." She reaches for her tea and takes a sip. "How are you feeling?"

I lean back against the couch. "Like I went to the biggest skatepark in the world, got pushed off the edge of the deepest bowl and didn't bail." Staring up at the ceiling, I imagine the vast universe beyond, and for the first time, I'm glad it chose me to be its messenger.

Dad flings open the door of his study. "Christ, Marvel, have you checked your phone? The press have been hounding me all morning. I'm not your bloody PA." He walks over to the window. "Shit. I'm not letting those vultures come anywhere near you."

"It's okay, Dad. This is nothing. It'll blow over."

"Doubt it. A teen psychic skateboarder makes great clickbait." Dad's phone rings. "Piss off! Oh, sorry, mate. Yeah, the press are being a pain in the arse." He looks at me. "She's up. Do you want to speak to her?" Dad listens for a few minutes. "Okay. Sure, I'll pass on the information. Can you send a car round? The slimeballs are trespassing again." He hangs up.

"Edmonds?"

"Yeah. Grant's admitted his role in Vince's kidnapping, the jeweller's murder and aggravated burglary. His fingerprints were all over the jewellery shop and Sadie's house. Fraud squad are looking into his business dealings. He transferred cash from his magazine business into bitcoin, to avoid losing it when *Edge* magazine went under."

I frown. "What about that large bitcoin payment Grant made? The one assumed to be hush money for Alex."

"Edmonds said Alex admits Grant promised him half the ransom money, but he denies receiving any bitcoin. "

"Yeah, right. Be interesting to see what happens to that stash of bitcoin once Alex gets out of jail."

Dad shrugs. "Grant manipulated Alex big time. Let the poor bugger keep it."

The doorbell rings, then someone raps on the lounge window and shouts, "Marvel, is it true you're psychic? Did you always know Grant was behind this?"

Dad swivels to the window. "Cheeky bastards. Stay there, Marvel."

Sadie arches an eyebrow. "Simon, just leave them, you'll only make things worse."

Dad ignores her and stomps over to the window. He yells through the glass, "Piss off, you're on private property. Cops will be here any minute."

An idea springs. A way to draw a line under everything and put an end to speculation. I head for the front door.

Dad's mouth hangs open. "Marvel?"

A group of seven or eight people surge towards me, cramming onto the doorstep. Cameras click and a flurry of questions fire from all directions. Someone shoves a microphone in my face.

I shout above the ruckus, "My father, Simon Harris is writing a full feature on the case including all the details about my psychic ability. It'll be on his blog tomorrow. There'll be no further comment from myself or my family."

Dad helps me close the door against the baying pack of media. He levels with me. "By tomorrow? You're one tough taskmaster." He grins. "I've already got the title: *Human error and bitcoin: How teen psychic, Marvel Harris rescued her kidnapped cousin and uncovered Grant Dickson's crimes.*"

"Hmm. Way too sensational. Can you tone it down?"

"Since when were you anointed my editor-in-chief?" His stern expression breaks into a smile. "Sure."

I charge up my phone. The screen comes alive, revealing pages and pages of missed calls and texts. Figuring he owes me a few favours, I phone Edmonds.

◆

A burly officer from Edmond's team escorts me through the gaggle of media congregating outside my house and into a waiting police car. I hop out around the corner from the drug rehab unit.

The two-storey building's bathed in afternoon sun and white flowers bloom from a glossy-leaved shrub by the entrance. Spring flowers mean one thing:

skateboarding. Months and months of good weather and tricks to master. Every Spring's a new beginning, a chance to become better than the last.

Vince is in the visitors' lounge. He jumps up off the couch and hugs me. "Marvel! You were on the news!"

I step back and admire his glowing skin and sparkling blue eyes. He's filled out a little bit too.

"You look fantastic."

"Yep, they've been feeding me up. All being well I'm out of here on Sunday. I've been so well supported." His speech gallops along on a wave of excitement, hopping from one subject to another. "Have you ever listened to TED talks? I'm addicted."

I smile. "No, but sounds like a good addiction to have."

"Cheeky." Vince grabs my arms and pulls me onto the couch. "No drugs or alcohol now for two weeks." He hesitates. "Though I wouldn't want to go through that first week again."

I shudder at the memory of him zip-tied to a chair.

"I've got this great counsellor. I was completely under Grant's spell." His eyes widen. "Can you believe what he did?" Sadness flickers across his face. "Is Sadie alright?"

"She's good. Staying with us for a few days." A deep sense of satisfaction comes over me at this profound shift in Vince's wellbeing, knowing that I helped him reach it.

"Did you hear about the new salon? Your dad helped me find it."

"No. I think Dad wanted you to tell me."

Vince throws out his hands. "It's my new start. I'm calling it Phoenix." He pauses. "You know, as in the mythological creature."

"I quite liked Bad Hair Daze." Hate to dampen his spirits, but I'm a sucker for a bit of wordplay.

Vince's face falls. "I was half-dead and rose from the bloody ashes." He splutters, "There's no going back to Bad Hair Daze."

I laugh. "I get the sentiment, Vince. I'm sure it'll grow on me."

"It's a tiny space and I'll be the only stylist." He smiles. "It's perfect."

His joy lifts my heart and makes the roller-coaster of the past few weeks worthwhile. "Dad says you're moving in with Sadie for a bit."

"Into the spare room—Mum's old room. How weird is that?" He hesitates, then his voice softens. "It's kind of nice, though."

His mention of Shirley prompts me to fill him in about Shirley's drawing and how she linked the skull ring to Grant all those years ago.

Vince sighs. "Everything's fated." He stares at me. "I'm so grateful to you. You saved me."

Tears well up and I hug Vince tight, so tight I can feel his heart beating against my chest. "You're family. I never gave up on you." I wipe away tears. "You might find this hard to believe, but you helped me too. A lot."

Vince searches my face. "Really?"

I nod and quickly change the subject. Last thing he needs is me bleating on about the past.

Vince chats about his plans for the future. Even mentions regaining his title of Hairdresser of the Year. He checks his watch. "Shit. I'm missing your Dad's show. I promised him I'd listen."

I grin. "My cue to leave, then." I kiss Vince's cheek. "Great to catch up."

He pulls on his headphones and gives me the thumbs up. "See you next week."

A text pings as I walk through the automatic doors. Noa's inviting me over later while his mum's at work. He follows the text with three black heart emojis. This time I go for it and fire a red heart emoji straight back.

CHAPTER TWENTY-THREE

Noa's front door is open. Cooking smells waft from the kitchen and from deeper inside the house, a TV blares. As I kick off my trainers, I swear I hear Emmeline's voice. Didn't Noa say she was working? Tension stiffens my limbs and I slowly straighten up, hoping I'm mistaken.

Teuila comes flying out of the lounge and squeals. She hugs me tight, her tiny arms just reaching around my hips. "I've missed you, Marvel. You haven't been over for ages." She steps back, looking at me with sad eyes.

"Sorry, Teuila. Things have been a bit crazy."

A slow grin forms. "Are you crazy about my brother?"

My cheeks burn.

Noa appears from the kitchen. His dark T-shirt is dusted with flour. "Teuila, stop pestering Marvel. Go help Mum."

Teuila pulls a face, then scurries into the kitchen, slamming the door behind her.

"Hi. Have you recovered from last night?" says Noa.

My voice cracks. "You told me your mum was working?"

He runs a hand through his hair. "I know, sorry. It's all okay, honestly."

"After everything that's happened, you may as well throw in damnation. It can't hurt."

He exhales. "Do you really think I'd invite you here to be damned?"

The hurt in Noa's eyes triggers a flicker of hope. *Has Emmeline changed her mind?*

Teuila's face appears around the kitchen door. "Mum wants to talk to you—just you." She points to me, then scampers off down the hallway.

My stomach lurches.

Noa sends me a reassuring look.

I wipe my palms on the back of my jeans and open the door. A blast of hot air hits me. Pots bubble on the hob, sending plumes of steam to the ceiling. A slab of meat rests in a roasting tray on the bench, juices pooling in the tin foil beneath it.

Emmeline stirs a pot of gravy with a wooden spoon. She lifts the spoon to her lips and takes a slurp, then throws in some salt.

My hands clench. It's like I'm back at St Joseph's again, waiting outside the Principal's office for another bollocking about daydreaming in class.

She stops stirring and turns to me. "I owe you an apology, Marvel. Your grandmother's a wonderful woman and so knowledgeable about visionaries in the Church." She pauses. "I was wrong to judge you."

A tide of relief floods over me. "Helping people is all I've ever tried to do."

"I know. I never gave you a chance, did I?" She looks sheepish. "Father Peter thinks very highly of your grandmother. He says you should think about attending Church sometime." She raises her eyebrows.

I bristle. "I'm afraid that won't be happening. There's a world of difference between spirituality and organised religion."

Emmeline gives a tight smile. She opens the oven door and beats away surging heat with a tea towel. "Right, potatoes done." She hauls a huge roasting tin out of the oven and plonks it on the bench. "Time to eat."

I relax back against the couch with a stomach full of delicious food. A cartoon plays on the TV and Noa beckons to me from the opposite couch where he's squashed between Tavita and Isaia. "I've something to show you."

Teuila blushes and sends me a furtive glance.

Inside Noa's shed the fug of paint fumes hits me, making my eyes water. "Can you open the window? It's intense in here."

Noa turns on the light, then pushes against the

latch of the cracked window pane. It doesn't budge. He applies more pressure, lurching forward as the window opens.

I breathe in fresh evening air.

"Sorry, it's the oils. I've been experimenting."

Noa's easel is covered with a filthy, paint-splattered cloth. The table below is littered with paintbrushes, half-full tubes of paint and a jar of dirty water.

Noa pushes loose curls behind his ears. "I'm a bit nervous." His hand hovers by the cloth, grasping it, then letting go. He takes a deep breath and whips it away.

I gasp. The sad expression in the eyes—my eyes—surprises me. Not because it isn't a true reflection, but because I thought I'd hidden it. He's shown the weight of responsibility I carry and my struggle with being different. Tears well up and I grab the chair below the easel and collapse into it, its rickety legs creaking underneath me.

Noa's face creases with worry and there's panic in his voice. "What is it? Don't you like it?"

"It's beautiful." Tears cascade down my cheeks, dripping into the jar of dirty water and onto paintbrushes.

His eyes bore into me, searching my face. "Then, why are you crying?"

"Sorry, it's just I didn't expect ..." I cover my face with trembling hands and mumble through my fingers. "I didn't expect it to *really* look like me."

Noa hesitates. "I don't just see your beauty, Marvel." He bends down and kisses my lips, sending my head into a whirl.

I stand up and pull him close. No way am I wasting this moment. The feelings I've buried burst out like a rush of adrenaline before a risky jump and I press my lips against his. Kissing Noa makes the outside world disappear and all that matters is his soft lips against mine. I slide my hand under his shirt and over smooth, warm chest. Even with the window open, sticky heat rises in the air around us.

"Shit. Sorry, Marvel." Noa grasps the back of the chair and lowers himself into it. "Ankle's playing up." He winces, then bursts out laughing. "Worst timing ever."

I hand him his crutches and smile. "I love the portrait and I lo—" My cheeks burn and I look at the floor. "I think you know how I feel."

Noa squeezes my hand. "Yep."

After saying goodbye to the children and thanking Emmeline, I walk with Noa to the end of his driveway. His kind eyes twinkle under the streetlight. How I underestimated the depths of what lay beneath them. I turn to him. "So, am I still Kandinsky?"

"Some things will never change. You'll always be Kandinsky." He hesitates and his gaze drifts into the distance. "You know, that portrait of you means a lot to me. It's easily the best work I've done since I painted Dad."

My eyes prickle with tears and I plant another kiss on his lips.

Faint cheering and whooping carries towards us.

Grateful for darkness hiding my hot face, I glance back to Noa's house.

The children clamour behind windows, banging on the glass and doubling up with laughter.

Noa grins and waves back to his siblings. "Our secret's out."

I give the children a wave, then meet Noa's eyes. "No going back now." I laugh. "They're already planning our wedding."

I skate home and it's like being continuously airborne, drifting in that semi-conscious moment between dream and reality. My lips tingle and I savour the memory of Noa's touch. Somehow, he delved into my soul and plastered it onto canvas. *Would he paint me differently now?*

Light streams from the lounge window onto the driveway, glinting against Dad's car. A takeaway coffee cup lies crumpled against the house, but there's no sign of any lurking media. Tomorrow, Dad's write-up will be released into the world, and knowing Dad, he won't pull any punches. The truth will be laid bare. It's about time.

CHAPTER TWENTY-FOUR

Mum thrusts a serving platter crammed with dips and crackers into my hands. "Can you take this to Sadie's?" She checks her watch. "Dad and I have to pick up Vince from the rehab unit." She wipes her hands down the front of her paint-flecked jeans. "I'd better go and get ready."

I pick one of Mum's long blonde hairs out of the smoked salmon dip and walk over.

A terracotta plant pot wedges open the front door and Sadie's house smells of lemon and fresh herbs. On the kitchen table is a cake decorated with the words *Welcome Home, Vince.*

Sadie takes the platter and finds space for it on the table next to bowls of salad and sliced meat. She looks up. "Follow me."

She shows me to the spare room. It's freshly painted and she's bought new bed linen and a lamp for the bedside table. Shirley's desk remains in the corner beneath the Rembrandt print, its oak surface gleaming in the sunlight. I remember my vision of her writing there and how her presence became a source of encouragement and reassurance. Was Shirley protecting Vince and me, like the guards in *The Night Watch* painting? Dragging Vince and me out of darkness into light?

"It's only till he gets back on his feet. I doubt Vince wants to live with his grandmother for too long," says Sadie.

I link her arm and walk back to the kitchen. "It's his new start. He's going to be fine."

Sadie hands me a cup of tea. "You seem happy."

"Thanks for speaking to Emmeline. I've risen up the ranks from devil worshipper to Catholic mystic."

"You're welcome. Father Peter had a word with her too. When I told him the psychic Emmeline was referring to was you, he was mortified." She hesitates. "And how's Noa? Still just friends?" A slow smile forms on her face.

I stifle a giggle. "I think you probably know the answer to that."

There's a knock on the front door. "Hello?"

The sound of Noa's voice shoots a thrill through me and I battle to compose myself.

Sadie starts rearranging cutlery. "Can you go?"

Noa's at the end of the hallway, leaning on his crutches. A huge bouquet of flowers bursts out from his open backpack.

Are they for me? That's super embarrassing. Not sure I'm into grand romantic gestures. "Hi. Nice flowers." I kiss his lips and pull away in case Sadie's watching. The flowers' sweet heady scent wafts across the hallway.

Noa looks awkward. "Actually, they're for your mum."

"Oh." My emotions swirl. A mixture of relief and mild disappointment.

"To say thanks."

I frown. "For what?"

Noa tilts his head and smiles.

I shout, "Oh my God. You got in!"

Noa beams. "Yep."

Sadie's heels click behind me. "What's happened? Are the press back again?" She pokes her head out of the front doorway, then turns to me.

"Noa got into Whitecliffe College."

Sadie's face lights up. "Oh, isn't that wonderful? Well done. And what beautiful flowers." She glances at me and smiles.

I laugh. "They're for Mum."

Sadie reaches for the flowers. "Here, I'll put them in some water."

Once Sadie's out of earshot, Noa leans in and kisses me on the lips. "I never had you down as a flowers kind of girl."

"Yep. Flowers and me are a total mismatch. They're so predictable and boring." Not wanting to sound ungrateful, I blurt, "Mum will absolutely love them, though."

"Hey, cuz." Luke bounds up the wooden steps and slaps Noa's back, then shakes his hand. "Sorry to break up you two lovebirds." He pecks me on the cheek, then steps back outside and wanders up and down the verandah, assessing the front of Sadie's house. "Sweet place." He makes a beeline for me. "You kept all that psychic stuff on the down-low, Marvel. It must drive you nuts." Luke's eyes lift over my head. "Oh, hello. You must be the lady of the house?"

Sadie's gaze wanders over Luke's dazzling white trainers, monogrammed polo shirt and the thick gold chain looping around his neck. "I've heard a lot about you, Luke. I'm Sadie, Marvel's grandmother. What a smart young man you are."

Noa and I exchange a look. We both know how that outfit was funded. An apprentice's wage will certainly put a dent in his clothing budget.

"Marvel tells me you're an electrician in training."

He grins. "Yep, bit of a career change." He flicks a light switch on and off. "If you need any electric work done on this place, give me a shout. I'll do you a sweet deal, even sweeter if you pay cash."

Sadie frowns. "Well, I'll certainly keep you in mind once you're properly trained."

The idea of Luke working with electricity fills me with unease. He *is* a live wire. I just hope he doesn't make a wrong connection and electrocute himself. I change the subject. "New starts all round, then."

Luke swivels to Noa. "You too?"

Noa nods. "Yep. I got into art school on a full scholarship."

"Nice one." Luke high fives Noa, then his face falls. "Cuz, your dad would be so proud."

I swallow and feel for Noa's hand, squeezing it tight.

Noa looks down. "Yeah, he would be. Thanks, Luke."

I pull out a chair from under Sadie's outdoor table and sit opposite Luke and Noa. Jasmine winds up support posts standing at the corners of the covered deck, its tiny buds close to bursting. A cool breeze drives away the sun's warmth, making me shiver, and in the distance, fast-moving clouds block sunlight, then drift past, allowing the sun's rays back through. It's a bittersweet day. A day unable to make up its mind, wandering up and down the temperature scale unsure where to go next, like it's reached a fork in the road.

Luke downs a glass of Coke and starts working his way through a bowl of Twisties, crunching one after the other, yet still managing to talk non-stop to Noa.

Every so often I catch Noa's eye and exchange a smile. I'm so happy for him and extremely relieved my mass destruction of his art portfolio didn't hold him back.

It's been a day since Dad's article hit. I'm getting tons of follow requests on Instagram and weird texts from randoms. Amazing who comes out of the woodwork once your name's in the news. Funny how the people who used to tear me to shreds about being psychic suddenly claim to have believed me all along. The most satisfying part is deleting the follow requests from the bullies at my old school. To hell with them.

A gust of wind catches the paper napkins on the table, sending them drifting onto the deck. I chase after them, scrunching up the soft paper before ditching them inside, into the kitchen bin. Voices carry from the hall. I turn towards them and a rush of emotion sweeps over me.

Vince stands at the far end of the hallway clutching a suitcase so tightly his knuckles are white.

Mum and Dad are on either side of him. Mum gently coaxes him towards the kitchen, while Dad tries to free the suitcase from Vince's iron grip. The bubbly Vince I chatted to in the rehab unit last week is taking his first steps back into real life, like a newbie skater learning where to position his feet.

He gives me a nervous smile.

I rush up.

He drops the suitcase and hugs me tight.

By the time Vince has let go, Mum and Dad have gone. Vince's gaze travels up and down the hallway, then back to me and I wonder if he's thinking the same thing as I am, that the ordeal he's been through was worth it.

Down in the kitchen, Mum shrieks with delight and a champagne cork pops. *Noa must've told her his news.*

I take Vince's arm and show him to his room.

He stands on the threshold and stares vacantly into the space. Eventually, he picks up the suitcase Dad left by the door and lays it on the bed, then sits at the desk where his mother used to write. "I feel like she's here with me." His voice trembles. "This house where she grew up. This room." He looks at me.

I whisper, "She's always with you, Vince." I pause. "Do you think you're up to facing everyone?"

"Yeah. Give me a few minutes." He smiles. "It's good to be out of rehab. It's just all a bit overwhelming."

Back in the kitchen, tinny music plays from Sadie's ancient stereo system, mixing with excited chatter from the deck outside.

Dad bounds in and angles the speakers to face outside, muttering about how shitty the stereo is. He's bought himself a new shirt in a plain charcoal grey. Maybe he's finally moving on from those awful band shirts.

Mum comes over and passes me a half-full flute of champagne. "Isn't it fabulous about Noa? He's got a wonderful future ahead of him." She clinks her glass against mine.

I take a sip. The bubbles fizz in my mouth, reminding me of how the last time I drank alcohol, at Mum's art exhibition, I ended up spewing.

Dad hollers to me, "Where's Vince?"

I glance up the hall. "He won't be long. He's just sorting out his stuff."

Mum pulls me to one side. "Any more fallout from your Dad's article?"

"No more reporters ambushing me, if that's what you mean." Edmonds put a stop to that. "Just getting lots of follow requests which I'm enjoying deleting."

"Did your father tell you he's been offered a regular column?"

I take a step back. "That's awesome."

I wave over to Dad. "You didn't tell me your news?"

He unravels a speaker cable. "Sorry, it's been a crazy twenty-four hours. I didn't expect the article to go viral. Thousands following me on Twitter now. As soon as you mention the word psychic, the nutters and God-botherers come out swinging." He reaches for his beer and takes a swig. "Makes me appreciate what you put up with at your old school."

Sadie walks in holding empty drinking glasses. "Yes, Simon, what do you call it again? A Tweet storm?"

I collapse into giggles.

Dad suppresses a laugh. "The preferred term is Twitter storm and I wouldn't go that far, Mother."

"Oh well. It's a bit of publicity for you, whichever way you look at it." Sadie deposits the glasses by the sink and wanders back outside.

Dad raises his eyes at me. "You and Noa an item?"

I cringe. "Yes."

"Well, your mother and I couldn't be happier. He's a lovely guy."

Emotion wells up. "Thanks, Dad."

Vince appears at the kitchen door. His watery eyes flick around the room and he's fidgety, sticking his hands in and out of the pockets of his cargo pants.

Sympathy pricks me and I go to his side and hand him a glass of fizzy apple juice.

Dad bellows from the corner, "Vince, come on through." He pulls out a drawer. "Mother, where's the bloody remote for this piece of cr—"

"For God's sake, Simon." Sadie passes the remote to Dad. She turns to Vince. "What can I get for you, Vince? You must be starving." She places his glass on the table and pushes a plate into his hands, piling it with salad, meat and crusty bread.

Vince stares at the growing pile of food on his plate, but doesn't say anything. I get the impression having a choice will take a bit of getting used to.

Sam Cooke's *Change is Gonna Come* plays and I shoot Dad a look. I know what he's doing here. The dodgy T-shirt may have gone, but it's a shame I can't say the same for his themed playlists.

Dad throws his hands out. "Took me ages, Marvel. It wasn't easy finding enough suitable songs." He cups a hand around his mouth, out of Vince's earshot and whispers, "Anything remotely drug or alcohol related was out."

I turn back to Vince, but he's wandered onto the outside deck and he's shaking Luke's hand. *Damn.* I meant to warn him Luke was coming. *What if he starts craving drugs at the sight of his old dealer?* I go over.

"Vince, you been chomping down the pies? You look great." Luke's voice cracks. "Last time I saw you, I honestly didn't think you'd make it."

Vince exhales. "Thanks. I've come a long way since then."

Luke holds Vince's gaze. "I regret selling you all those dr—" He bites his lip. "I got involved with the wrong crowd. The money sucked me in."

Vince puts his plate down and drapes his arm around Luke's shoulders. "I was addicted long before I met you."

Bowie's *Changes* comes on the stereo. I catch Noa's eye and grit my teeth.

He laughs and pats the empty seat beside him.

I huddle up close to Noa.

He reaches around my waist and pulls me closer. "So, what's next for Marvel Harris?" His eyes flick to the sky. "More adventures?"

I shake my head. "This was the adventure of a lifetime and I hope nothing like this *ever* happens again."

Noa looks surprised. "Are you still getting visions?"

"Yeah. Every few days." I'd bore him to death if I told him about every single one. "Everything's calmer now. There's no scary stuff coming through." Spirits used me to fix broken lives and now there's nothing to mend. And if I'm brutally honest, one of those broken lives was mine.

Mum appears with the cake and places it on the table, in front of Vince.

Sadie follows, holding plates and a cake slice.

Dad turns down the music, then stomps onto the deck and taps a teaspoon against a glass of champagne. He clears his throat. "I just want to say a few words. It's great to have Vince home and back in the family. We've missed you, mate."

Vince's lower lip trembles.

"Thanks to Noa for supporting Marvel, despite being on those bloody crutches, and well done for getting a place at art school." Dad turns to Luke. "Good to finally meet you, Luke. Not many people have the balls to chase a kidnapper, search a jewellery shop under pressure and knock out an armed man. Thanks, mate. And one piece of advice for your fledgling career as a sparky: *always* remember the earth wire."

Luke stands and takes a bow.

Dad hesitates, then glances to me. "And that brings me to you, Marvel." He swallows and looks down.

Mum shuffles to Dad's side and links his arm.

A lump forms in my throat.

"You knew those damn visions were trying to tell you something and it's a testament to your character that you didn't give up, even though you were scared shitless. And once you found Vince, you continued to search for the truth." He looks across to me with teary eyes. "I've never been happy about you being psychic.

Life's hard enough as it is." He sighs. "But I'm slowly coming round to the idea that it is a Gift rather than a curse."

Dad's eyes meet mine and I try to speak but I can't. It's a shock to know he's been struggling to come to terms with me being psychic too. *Maybe there was actually a time when Dad wasn't always angry with the world?*

Dad raises his glass. "To Vince, his new salon, and moving in with his gran at twenty-five."

Laughter rings out.

Sadie feigns offence and raises her glass. "Welcome home, Vince."

Mum presents Vince with a painting. "I created this especially for you. A reminder of how far you've come. It's called *Love and Redemption*."

Vince looks stunned. He holds the painting with stiff arms and stares at the canvas. Eventually, he turns it around to face the table. The lower half consists of black wavy lines with tiny slashes of orange in-between them. Above this section, thick swirls of white, orange and yellow intertwine like a raging bonfire. I'm transfixed by the painting and I realise this is the first time one of Mum's paintings has communicated something meaningful.

Noa leans towards the painting. "Julia, it's beautiful. Great form and depth of colour."

"I love it." Vince sniffs. "It's the first piece of art I've ever owned." I get the impression there's going to be a lot of firsts for Vince in the next few months.

My legs are restless. All the emotion of the day has stockpiled me with nervous energy and it's reaching tipping point. I knock over Noa's glass by accident, spilling Coke onto Sadie's white tablecloth.

"Are you alright?" Noa looks me in the eyes. "Go out for a bit on your board. I'll make up an excuse for you." He dabs at the Coke with a bunch of paper napkins.

"Okay. Thanks." With Noa's encouragement, my obligation to stay crumbles and I give in to the urge to skate. And when no one's looking, I slip out.

I count down the different-coloured garden gates as I jog up the street. Each gate I pass brings me closer to the top of the hill. New leaves burst from trees lining the road and birds flit within their branches. Days are getting longer. Summer's on its way.

I reach the orange gate—the last one—and my anticipation soars. I pull off my backpack and take a few swigs from my water bottle while I wait for my breathing to settle. I wipe my sweat-slicked forehead with my sleeve.

Below me, on the opposite side of the road, is Sadie's white villa. My house lies hidden behind hers, in its own private world. Further along the street is the tree where Noa fell. At the base of the tree, where pavement is ruptured by growing roots, weeds sprout from the cracks. The same cracks that tripped up Noa.

Memories from that day flood back. His blood stark against my pale skin, its redness like the glistening ruby eyes of the skull ring. And the way his pure white aura magnetised me. I know this sounds really lame, but he's been like a guardian angel to me ever since that day.

Taking a final slug of water, I wait until traffic clears. One foot firmly on the pavement, I hang my skateboard over the kerb and steady it with my other foot. My heart rate's on the ascent and adrenaline pumps through my veins like rocket fuel. Nothing beats the prospect of hurling myself down a steep hill, into a minefield of risk and hazard, just for kicks. After all the twists and turns of the past few weeks, it's good to know danger hasn't lost its edge.

"One, two, three!" I crash onto the road and pound my foot against asphalt, then crouch down low. My rolling wheels disturb the tranquillity of the street, injecting life into this sleepy suburb. The first speed bump looms and it's the one with the steepest run-up. My eyes narrow and I push my foot against the road, gaining maximum speed. My skateboard wobbles with my shifting weight, but I'm in control and on track. My wheels roll faster, noisier and air rips past me, billowing out my shirt. Then nothing, no sound, just me floating. Airborne at last.

ACKNOWLEDGEMENTS

This book (and everything that influenced it) could not have happened without:

The support of Creative New Zealand and the New Zealand Society of Authors.

The mentorship of Mandy Hager.

The structural editing, wisdom and support of Brandi Dixon (charcoalandbrass.co.nz).

My early teachers, Raewyn Alexander and Janice Marriott.

Sue Copsey's skill as a copy editor.

My mum, for teaching me to read before I started school.

My dad, for buying me a reading book every week from the newsagent.

Growing up in a grim Northern town. Finding friends who shared the same sense of humour, taste in music and desire to escape.

The support of my family in New Zealand and the UK. Special thanks to my parents, Marion and John,

Ian, Mo, Alistair, Kieran and Adam for their love, support and encouragement.

My cousin, the artist Alison Edmonds, for answering my questions about Art.

Detective Senior Sergeant Geoff Baber and John Dustow for help with research.

Jim McWilliams' advice about skateboarding.

My friend, and psychic, Lyn-Marie; your experiences helped bring Marvel to life.

All the friends who've encouraged me, read my stories and made me laugh.

Mark, Joe, Frankie and Rosa. This writing life couldn't exist without you.

ABOUT THE AUTHOR

Sarah M Bailey is a doctor and writer. Originally from the UK, she emigrated to Auckland, NZ with her family in 2008. In 2020, she was awarded a mentorship with the NZ Society of Authors. *Believing In Marvels* is her debut novel.

For more information about the author and to keep informed about future book releases, please go to sarahmbailey.com

www.ingramcontent.com/pod-product-compliance
Lightning Source LLC
Chambersburg PA
CBHW021120110726
47900CB00007B/2270